Flurry the Bear

The Land of the Sourpie

J.S. Skye

Flurry the Bear

The Land of the Sourpie

2nd Edition – January 2015
First Published – February 2013

All characters featured in this novel, the distinctive names and likenesses thereof, and all related content are the sole property of J.S. Skye. No similarity between any of the names, characters, persons, and/or institutions in this book with those of any living or dead person or institution is intended, and any such similarity which may exist is purely coincidental.

The Land of the Sourpie
(Flurry the Bear – Book 2)
Copyright © 2015 J.S. Skye
All rights reserved.
www.FlurryTheBear.com

Cover art by Luís Figueiredo, J.S. Skye, & Tony Washington

ISBN: 0692371850
ISBN-13: 978-0692371855

CONTENTS

CONTENTS

CHAPTER 1
A SPECIAL INVITATION

Golden rays beamed through Flurry's bedroom window. The melody of birds clearly carried upon the wind, as if the room were without walls. From the small, framed aperture, lush greenery extended as far as the eye could see. Only rich blue hues, broken by cotton-like clouds, contrasted the expanse of foliage that encircled such a quaint abode. The beauty of new life was ever abundant. Fresh growth saturated everything in sight from the newly-budded trees, the trimmed lawn, to the vibrant flowers that lined the house. Flurry sat up from his pillow, pulled away the sheets, rubbed his eyes, and then stretched out his arms with a hearty yawn. It was a new day, and Flurry was not about to miss it. The gorgeous outdoors was new to the young cub. He had only known winter before, so it was a treat to see something new.

Three months had passed since his arrival in Middleasia. Flurry had quickly settled into his new life in the cozy little town of Haengbokville, but he still missed all of the fun in the snow back in his homeland of Mezarim.

In the days that followed Flurry's exodus from the North Pole, he learned of many new things. He was introduced to his new favorite food, spaghetti – though he pronounced it as p'sghetti. He also experienced the joy of delicious chocolate milk. Back in the village of Ursus, Flurry always loved hot chocolate the most – drinking it cold had never crossed his mind. Chocolate milk was now, by far, Flurry's beverage of choice. You could always tell he had been drinking it, due to his signature chocolate mustache that he proudly displayed across his upper lip. Against his pure, white fur its contrast made his activity overtly apparent to anyone.

Despite his new favorites, Flurry generally liked foods of every kind – after all, what bear does not? Flurry loved to eat. Eating was the second most important thing in Flurry's life, besides himself. He made sure that he took priority over everything else. Overcoming his pride issue was anything but easy. After all, he truly was the cutest teddy bear in existence – or so he liked to tell himself. In fact, Flurry regarded himself as one of the most humble, and he made sure to let everyone know.

Even though he had been sent away from his family in Ursus, to learn a lesson in humility, Flurry still thought very highly of himself. He continued to admire his good looks and would often get caught adoring himself in the mirror. His actions would lead to being given a lecture or getting grounded if he were found to be too prideful or adoring himself excessively.

Flurry's new mother and father were human, and they treated him very well – as if he were their own son. He felt like he was their very own child, and he deeply loved them in return. However, despite the love of his new life, he still missed his teddy bear parents up at the North Pole. Christopher Kringle had promised that Flurry could visit from time-to-time, when permitted. To Flurry, that decree seemed like ages ago.

A lot had happened since his time away from Ursus. Flurry gained new friends to play with, and enlist to go on adventures together in the back yard. A tall, slender lion named Noah had become Flurry's best friend. Despite not having a mouth, Noah was certainly Flurry's favorite of the two lion cubs. It was highly probable that Flurry's choice came down to which of the two lion cubs would allow him to speak the most.

Boaz, the second of the two lions, often kept to himself. This wee cub, with his bushy mane that covered his ears, loved to learn. Knowledge was his friend – no, his passion. This fervor for knowledge always dwarfed any desire he might have had to go play with Flurry and the others. He was not anti-social by any stretch of the imagination, but playing was not always a priority to him. He could often be found wearing his reading glasses, plopped down behind a book – one much more sizeable than him, more often than not.

Caboose, on the other hand, was never far from Flurry. In fact, this little polar bear was with Flurry so often that you could mistake him for Flurry's shadow – if only Caboose would have had black fur instead of his vanilla ice cream hue. Caboose looked up to and admired Flurry too much to be away from him for very long. Anything Flurry would tell Caboose was taken to heart and accepted without question – after all, why would Flurry ever say anything that Caboose could not trust? Some would say the polar bear's blind trust was foolish, but to the lady of the house, she found it to be quite endearing.

As for Honja, what is there to say about this exceptionally miniscule rabbit? With his dark, brown fur, he was frequently mistaken for a mouse – something which he strongly resented. Honja had always been the loner of the group. He did not like to socialize with the others very much. Instead of mingling with his brothers, he would lose himself in his music collection. Either listening to his headset or playing games that did not require other participants, Honja kept himself entertained in his own way. It could be assumed that because Honja could not speak English that this language barrier was why he kept to himself. However, he could speak with Boaz or their human mother any time he wanted to, since they both understood him. Regardless of the situation, Honja often had an attitude that kept everyone at a distance – to say "grumpy" would be an understatement.

They each had unique character traits that made them stand out from one another. They were all very good friends and generally enjoyed each other's company – though they all found themselves annoyed with Flurry more often than not.

Noah had always been the voice of reason among the gang – as ironic as that may sound, considering that Noah was without a mouth. Flurry, being so young, rarely, if ever, listened to Noah or anyone else.

All of the members of this plush gang found it invigorating to play and explore in the back yard. It was amazing how many adventures they could find for themselves despite the small, confined space of the yard. However, if Flurry was anything, it would certainly be innovative. He liked to say that he took after his daddy in that regard.

Living in Haengbokville was pleasant and peaceful, especially in the spring. Flurry loved to play in the water puddles after a fresh rain shower. Rolling in the grass, swimming in the pool, and watching the butterflies flutter about were also new experiences for him. So many people take such things for granted, but not Flurry – nor Caboose for that matter. Caboose was especially enamored with just about everything.

These new experience were like opening a birthday gift, and Flurry loved receiving gifts almost as much as he loved food.

Flurry was often reminded that his new life was supremely better than what he had left behind back in his own world. Yet, amidst the fun and excitement of his new life in Haengbokville, Flurry pined for the days of getting into trouble with his friend Sunny. He longed to go sledding with his cousin Bliz. He even missed getting scolded by his school teacher – as crazy as that sounds.

Although he had a fun-filled season with all of the wonders and joy of eating ice cream, licking popsicles, and going to the playground, Flurry still preferred the snow.

Each day had passed just like the one

before it – slowly, from Flurry's point of view. Yet, this day was different. Little did Flurry know that a special surprise awaited him in the mailbox. Flurry sat on the hardwood floor in the bedroom and played a board game with Noah and Caboose. As usual, Caboose was right at Flurry's side. Anywhere Flurry went, Caboose would always tag along. Honja and Boaz were nowhere to be found – as was their custom.

While Flurry was in the midst of rolling the dice, there was a knock at the door. "Who is it?" Flurry called out as he tossed the numbered cubes to the game board.

"Flurry, a letter came in the mail for you. It's from ... the North Pole?" Flurry's mother informed him with a hint of curiosity in her tone.

Flurry could not have gotten up fast

enough. He launched himself toward the door as if he were a living rocket. His mother opened the door and handed the envelope to her giddy boy. Flurry did not waste any time opening it. After he ripped the letter out of its packaging, he stood there and looked at the letter while everyone waited eagerly to hear what it said. Even Boaz and Honja came out of hiding for this.

Now, Flurry always liked to act more grown up than he actually was. He was certainly smart, for only being a teddy bear cub, but he still could not read very well. He continued to stand in place with his gaze fixed upon the letter. He did not want to look silly for not knowing what the letter said, but he did not know what to do. In an attempt to look smart, Flurry said, "Wow! What a great letter! You guys should read it, too!"

Flurry's mother, being pretty bright, knew what Flurry was doing. She humored him by interjecting, "Wow! You're such a big bear, now! I'm so proud of you! Would you like me to read it to the rest of them?" Seeing through Flurry's act, she decided to help him save face in front of the others.

The young oriental lady stood over the cub with an outstretched arm. Flurry handed her the letter and with a tone of indifference replied, "Sure, I suppose." Internally he was pleased that she saved him from a potentially embarrassing situation, but he knew how to play it cool.

Adjusting her glasses, Flurry's mother raised the letter to eye level and began to read: "Dear Flurry, everyone has been asking about you. It's not surprising that you're deeply missed by us all. It has been over three months since you were last here. We've spoken to the villagers, and they would like for you to come visit for a few days. Your parents miss you more than words can relay. You may bring your friends if you'd like. They would be very welcome here. While you're here, be sure to pick up any of your things that you would like to take back with you. All of us hope to see you soon. A package will arrive shortly to allow you to travel here faster. We look forward to seeing you soon. Yours truly, Christopher & Catherine."

Flurry was so excited. He jumped up and down and gave Noah a big hug. "Can you believe it? I get to go home! Yay!" Flurry kept jumping while the other plush animals cheered with him. Their mother stood over them all with an amused smile. "So, who wants to come with me?" the cub asked.

Boaz shouted out, "Me!" followed by Caboose saying, "I do!"

Noah would have said something if he could speak, but instead he held up a sign that conveyed the message that he was also onboard with the idea.

Honja said something in his native tongue, but Flurry was unable to understand him. None of the cubs, save Boaz, had yet learned to speak Honja's language. However, judging from the rabbit's body language and tone, he seemed enthusiastic about joining Flurry, too. This was indeed a special occasion, because it was rare that the word "enthusiastic" and "Honja" could be used in the same sentence.

"Good! Let's go!" Flurry exclaimed as he

rushed over to his nightstand to make preparations for the trip.

"Well, hold on there a minute!" commanded Flurry's mother. "We have to make sure you're well fed before you go. We'll have to pack some winter clothes, and some food for the trip. By the way, how are you going to get there?"

Flurry, being so sure of himself, answered, "Oh, Mommy, you're so silly! I know how to get there."

Flurry's mother was not convinced by his answer, so she tried to dig deeper. "Flurry, you didn't answer my question. How are you going to get there?"

"It's easy!" Flurry assured her. Then he looked from side-to-side, and put his paw to the side of his mouth before whispering, "I can't tell you. It's a secret."

Though Flurry was sincere in his statement, it was only half true. The truth was that it was indeed a secret to anyone not from the land of Mezarim. Anyone that would dare travel to the North Pole in our world would find nothing there but snow, ice, frigid temperatures, and polar bears. To the uninitiated, it would appear to be a barren sheet of ice. However, there is a passageway that is invisible to the naked eye. When passed through, this hidden gateway would reveal an entire world previously unseen. Very few have ever truly seen the North Pole as it actually existed. What is really at the North Pole has been cleverly disguised from the outside world.

However, as I said, Flurry's statement was not entirely true. In fact, the false part of it was when he mentioned going to the

North Pole to be easy. It may have been for him, once he received the package that the Kringle family promised in the letter, but not typically so for others. After passing through the hidden gateway, the land is full of dangers and obstacles. The northern region is protected by an army of warrior elves that allied themselves with Christopher Kringle many ages ago and now guard the land from invading enemies and other dangers.

Flurry was aware of the dangers, but also knew that his own mode of transportation involved an item that arrived in a package later that day. In fact, there was an entire incident accompanied by that box, but that is a story for another time.

They were all excited and as worked up as children can get. Flurry rambled on and on about how wonderful the North Pole was and how much fun they would have. Flurry told them about everything he could think of, and it only added another log to the fire of anticipation that burned within each of them.

The rest of the day went by like a bolt of lightning. Throughout its course, they had gotten their bags all packed and ready to go for the following morning. Flurry had done many things that day, but his mind had been constantly consumed by his excitement to return to his home village. Not surprisingly, Flurry's mind gravitated toward memories of the delicious food in Ursus, more specifically Mrs. Kringle's chocolate chip cookies. Flurry loved her cookies so much, and his mouth watered as he thought about how chewy and delicious they were.

The evening quickly came, and they all

nestled in their beds. As they each slid under their blankets, their mother came around and tucked them in with a parting kiss on the cheek. "I'll see you in the morning," she said. After she had finished tucking them in, she walked to the door, turned back for a moment and called to them, "Good night! I love you! Sweet dreams!"

They all replied in their own unique manner. Honja replied in his language, Noah waved, and the other three replied, "I love you, too!"

Flurry got the final word in when he closed the dialogue off by saying, "Okay, good night!" On that statement, Flurry's mother flipped off the lights and shut the door.

After the door latched shut, Flurry laid there in bed, and peered out into the darkness of the room. He was too excited to sleep. He imagined a grand welcoming party and all of the tasty treats he would indulge in. He could not wait to make snow angels, build snowbears, go sledding, and have snowball fights with Noah and the others. As Flurry continued to fantasize about their next day, he drifted off to sleep and had dreams of fun and exciting adventures.

The next morning Flurry jumped out of bed and ran to the door with his bag in tow. In the haste of his departure, he blew past his mother as she sat at the computer desk in the far corner of the room. "Where do you think you're off to in such a hurry?" she inquired of him.

Flurry had not noticed her presence and was startled at the sound of her voice. He spun around, backed up against the closed bedroom door, and stood there petrified. With his arms behind his back, as he usually stood when he was guilty of something, he answered her. "I was just testing my backpack to make sure it stays secure, in case we have to run from danger."

He looked up and grinned uneasily at her. As cute as he was, he did not fool her at all. "Flurry, first of all, you didn't make your bed," she started.

"Oops! Sorry!" Flurry replied as he sprinted back over to the bed and put the bedspread back in place.

"Secondly, were you running off without waking up your brothers?" she asked in a concerned tone.

"Oops!" Flurry giggled, and with an embarrassed tone continued. "Yeah, I thought I was forgetting something. Now I know what it was."

"Hey, Noah! Time to get up!" Flurry shouted as he shook Noah vigorously by the shoulders.

Noah leapt up at once, but when he beheld Flurry an expression of anger fell upon his face. Noah grabbed a tablet of paper and wrote something down. He then held it up for Flurry to read the inscription: "Flurry! GO AWAY!" Though Flurry could not read, he could make out his name and see how irate Noah appeared to be.

Flurry giggled nervously and said, "Oops! Sorry, Noah." Flurry then raced off to Caboose's bedside.

In an attempt to prevent the same thing from happening three more times, his mother called out to her teddy bear cub. "Flurry! Stop! This time, be more subtle and gentle in waking the others. Don't startle them like you did with Noah. Okay?" Flurry's mother foresaw conflict on the horizon if Flurry did the same thing to Honja.

"Sorry, Mommy," Flurry answered. At Caboose's bedside, Flurry gently nudged Caboose's shoulder and whispered, "Caboose. Caboose. Your turn to get up."

Despite Flurry's attempt to be very quiet and subtle, Caboose shot straight up in bed and yelled, "I'm not a turnip!"

At first, Flurry was stunned and did not know what to say. Then he giggled and said, "What are you talking about?"

Caboose looked around, still with a startled look on his face. "Oh, nussing. I was just dreaming," he answered. In addition to having a very soft, whistle-like voice,

Caboose pronounced words that contained "th" as if they had an "s" instead. So when he said "nothing", it sounded like he said "nussing."

Flurry could not quit giggling. He tried his best to keep silent, but he just could not keep the laughter inside. It was exactly like one of those moments in a quiet place like a library or a church when you knew you should not laugh, but no matter how hard you tried, you could not contain it. Well, this was exactly how Flurry felt. He tried to hold his breath, cover his mouth, and even bury his head in the pillow. However, the giggling would not stop.

Noah shook his head to and fro, as if he knew what was coming next. Noah reached for his headset and put it over his ears. He was prepared for the inevitable.

Flurry knew that he should keep quiet, so that he would not startle Boaz or Honja. Try as he might, Flurry could not contain the laughter building up inside of him. It was like he could explode at any moment. Flurry looked at Caboose again and said, "You're not a turnip? Hee, hee, hee, hee, hee! You're not a turnip? Hee, hee, hee, hee, hee! That's good to know, Caboose!" Flurry continued to giggle. "I always wondered about that," he added in jest.

Flurry's face looked as if it were being filled with hot air. His cheeks puffed out, and then it was too late. Flurry's hysteria came bursting forth. He laughed so hard that he fell on the floor and rolled around, kicking his legs back and forth. Flurry's glee reached the ears of Boaz and Honja, which abruptly ripped from their slumber.

"Flurry! See what you did?" His mother exclaimed in an angry tone. She did not receive an answer. Flurry laughed so hard that his eyes filled with tears.

As he rolled around on the ground, he kept repeating the phrase, "I'm not a turnip! Ha, ha, ha, ha, ha! I'm not a turnip! Ha, ha, ha, ha, ha!"

Caboose smiled and soon joined Flurry in the merriment. Noah shook his head again, as if he were witnessing something very typical of Flurry.

Honja and Boaz were still confused about what was going on. "Mommy, what's wrong with Flurry?" Boaz asked, clearly annoyed.

"I don't know, Sweetie. I think Flurry didn't get enough sleep last night," she replied.

"Flurry! Stop being so weird!" Boaz

pleaded.

Honja looked irritated and pulled his pillow down over his head.

Eventually things were under control. Flurry had mostly calmed down, though he had some giggles from time-to-time while they got ready for the day. As the sun progressed across the sky Flurry would occasionally make a remark or call out for Caboose, but he would shout, "Hey Turnip!" instead of using Caboose's real name.

The boys got their gear together, and their mother helped them with their bags after she had slipped some food into each one. Their mother looked at all of them with tears in her eyes as she spoke. "All of you take care of each other, and be safe. Flurry, make sure you look after them. You're responsible if anything happens to them."

"Don't worry, Mommy, I've got it all under control," Flurry said in a confident voice while he bore a smug look on his face.

Noah shook his head. He knew full well how irresponsible Flurry could be. Flurry's mother was still wary. Since she knew this same fact about Flurry, she turned to Noah and whispered to him, "Noah, keep an eye on them for me. I know I can count on you. Don't let Flurry do anything foolish. Okay?"

Noah nodded his head to show that he would watch over them. Noah was much more dependable than the others. He was a lot more mature and level-headed than all of the rest of them combined – you could say he had wisdom beyond his years.

After they were all geared up and ready to go, Flurry's mother opened the front door for them. She turned back to look when she heard Flurry's voice in the distance. He had not gone out the door, but she heard him shout, "Okay, goodbye!" Perplexed, she noticed they were no longer in the same room with her.

Where did they go? she wondered. The lady of the house closed the front door and walked through the house in search of her boys. As she came into their bedroom, she noticed clues that led her to conclude that they had gone into the closet. *That's strange!* she thought to herself. *Why would they do that?* She opened the door, but there was not a single trace of her cubs. It was as if they had vanished into thin air.

CHAPTER 2
AN UNPLEASANT SURPRISE

Having been brought to life, miraculously, by Christopher Kringle, some residual effects had clung to Flurry without anyone being aware of it. Though unintended, Christopher Kringle had been suspicious that something unique had happened with Flurry, so he kept a close eye on the cub. Due to this happenstance, Flurry had mysterious powers without any knowledge of this fact. This enabled him to lead his friends through the closet and instantly find themselves in Ursus, via the device found in the parcel that had arrived the night before.

Late the previous evening, Flurry opened the mysterious package to find what appeared to be nothing more than a door handle. It seemed like a very odd object for Mr. Kringle to send him. There were only two of such a device in existence; the other one was used by none other than Kringle himself.

Flurry learned how to operate the device from the included instructions. Boaz was of great help to Flurry in this regard. The guide indicated that travel between two locations could be done by merely thinking of a desired destination and placing the handle against any flat surface. At the turn of the decorative lever, the surface would become a doorway to whichever place Flurry's mind focused on.

The other fuzzies tried to use it, but to no avail. What made this object special was that it would not work for anyone else but Flurry, due to his unique origin. Even Flurry did not understand how this ability was so. As far as he was concerned, he could do it simply because he was awesome – though you and I know better.

After the short moment it took for Flurry and his friends to travel to Ursus, they were greeted by the entire teddy bear community. At the entrance to the teddy bear village they all stood, too numerous to count. The crowd cheered and waved at Flurry and his friends as they drew near.

At the forefront of the crowd stood Flurry's teddy bear parents, Mr. and Mrs. Snow. Behind his parents stood Mr. and

Mrs. Kringle, along with Flurry's other family members. Flurry ran up to his mama and gave her a hug. Tears streamed down their faces as Flurry's papa joined in a group hug.

After a period of prolonged tears and affection, Flurry's mama asked, "Son, are you going to introduce us to your friends?"

"Oh, yeah! Sorry about that. Mama, Papa, this is Noah, Boaz, Honja, and Caboose, but he prefers to be called 'Turnip'," Flurry giggled.

"Yeah!" Caboose nodded, but when he realized that he had agreed to the name "Turnip" he quickly corrected himself. "Hey! Sat's not my name!"

Flurry cackled and then continued with his introduction "They're my new friends from Middleasia. We share a room together.

Noah's my best friend!" The crowd listened in on Flurry's exposition – not that Flurry was trying to be private. He always liked to be the center of attention.

"It's nice to meet you," Flurry's parents kindly greeted his friends.

Then Flurry rushed up to Mr. Kringle, who had been standing there observing the entire interaction. Flurry tugged on Christopher's pant leg. "Come here! Come here!" Flurry exclaimed, while he attempted to draw Christopher closer to his friends.

Flurry then rushed up to Noah and the others and shouted, "Do you know who this is? Well, do you?"

Caboose scratched his head, while he sported a dumbfounded look on his face, and then shrugged.

Noah shook his head back and forth to

indicate that he, too, did not know.

Boaz and Honja were not amused with Flurry's antics, which resulted in Boaz sighing before he answered, "I'm sure you're going to tell us."

Flurry shouted, "It's Santa!"

Flurry's pals looked at one another and back at Flurry again. Then Boaz replied, "Okay?" It was evident that the name did not ring a bell for anyone in Flurry's gang.

Flurry felt exasperated as he thought to himself, *How could they not know who Santa is?* Flurry addressed his roommates again, "Guys! You know? The one that brings presents on Christmas Eve!"

At this time, Mr. Kringle cleared his throat and directed his statement toward Flurry's brothers, "It's Christopher Kringle actually. San'ta is the Polarin word for father." Christopher turned toward Flurry and continued. "Flurry, not everyone knows about me. You can explain everything later. In the meantime, welcome home! I hope you'll enjoy the next few days here. Make the most of it!"

Christopher and Catherine waved goodbye, left the crowd, and strolled down the cobblestone path that led back toward the southeastern part of the small town. Their large stone home could be seen in the distance. As the young couple departed, Flurry wanted to follow along. The cub's mother grabbed him by the paw and led him along with the rest of Flurry's company. "Come, now. We should head home for a meal, and while we're at it, there's someone I'd like for you to meet."

"Who? Who is it, Mama?" Flurry

inquired.

"You'll see. Just be patient." Mrs. Snow led Flurry up the path, followed by his friends and his papa, who brought up the rear of their caravan.

They arrived at the front door of the home where Flurry grew up – if you could say that about a teddy bear that never aged. The light brown-colored house was the same as he remembered it, with the same blue shutters and front door that sported the two-snowflake family crest. The fireplace had already been lit, and smoke ascended from the chimney.

The front door opened, just as they strode up the path. At the threshold was a petite, cream-colored teddy bear that stepped out from the warm interior and into the cold. She had a cute blue nose, a blue dress, and

two blue bows in the fur upon her head –
one above each ear. She was simply
adorable! Her cute looks quite possibly
rivaled that of Flurry's – something that
would not go over well with him.

Flurry looked at her, perplexed. He
thought he had met all of the teddy bears in
Ursus, but he did not have any memory of
this particular one. Flurry continued to study
her as they approached. Then Flurry noticed
the snowflakes on her dress. These
snowflakes were unmistakable – they were
the Snow family's crest. *Could she be a
distant cousin that I haven't met?* Flurry
thought to himself.

Mr. and Mrs. Snow helped everyone
inside. While they shook the snow off of
their feet, Flurry walked up to the female
bear. He looked her over, but did not say a

word. Flurry stood and gazed at her. He seemed suspicious as he inspected the young cub. Much like Flurry would do, she put her arms behind her back and blushed a bit while she looked uneasy. The female cub exchanged concerned glances with Mrs. Snow.

Mrs. Snow quickly intervened and said, "Flurry, I want you to meet Fall. She has been so excited to see you. We told her all about you. Isn't this exciting? You have a little sister."

Flurry froze in place with his mouth ajar. His face would have been as white as a sheet, if his fur were not already white. It took a moment for the shock to wear off enough for him to say, "Sister? Sister? Since when? I don't have a sister! I never had a sister! This can't be true!" Flurry shouted with indignation in his voice. "I don't want a sister! Mama, I thought you only loved me!"

Flurry ran up the steps to his old bedroom, flopped onto the bed, and cried.

Downstairs, Mr. Snow looked at Mrs. Snow, shrugged, and said, "Well, I think that went a lot better than we anticipated."

Mrs. Snow sighed. "I should go see if he's okay. In the meantime, Fall, acquaint yourself with Flurry's friends. I'll be right back." Mrs. Snow rushed off to attend to her son.

"Hello. I'm Fall," the young teddy bear softly spoke to the others.

"Hello," the dinky lion replied. "I'm Boaz, the other lion is Noah; the polar bear is Caboose, and the ..." Before Boaz could finish, Fall had already interrupted.

"Awww! What a cute little mouse!" Fall

exclaimed as she bent down and patted Honja on the head.

Honja was instantly upset, pushed her paw away from his head, turned his back to her, and crossed his arms.

"Now, you did it!" Boaz exclaimed. "He hates being patted on the head, and he really hates being mistaken for a mouse. He's a bunny rabbit."

"Oh! I'm sorry! I didn't mean to make you angry, little bunny." Fall tried to smooth the matter over.

"His name is Honja," Boaz added.

"Little Honja, please don't be mad. If you will forgive me, I'll give you some of my cookies. My mama made them for me, and I'll share them with you." Fall attempted to bribe the bunny's forgiveness.

Surprisingly, it worked. Flurry had never

been that clever at winning Honja over, but Fall had now succeeded where Flurry failed – though it is doubtful that Flurry ever really tried very hard. Teddy bears do hold tasty treats in high regard.

Honja turned around and was met by Fall's paw which held a cookie out for him. He tried to act disinterested, but he gave in and quickly nibbled away at the baked treat. The sweet-tasting pastry was as big as he was, if not larger. The bunny was quite content and had already forgotten the mistaken identity. As far as Honja was concerned, he now liked Fall better than Flurry. If there had been a vote, Honja would have elected Flurry out of office.

"Wow! That's amazing!" Boaz exclaimed. "I've never seen Honja's anger get squelched so easily. You have a gift.

Maybe you can come back with us, and Flurry can stay here."

"Thank you! I think?" Fall answered with a moment of caution and then a giggle.

"What's a squelch?" asked Caboose.

"No, Caboose. It's not a 'thing'. It means to stop or suppress," Boaz explained.

"Ohhh! I like supper!"

"No! Not supper! I said … oh, never mind."

Fall's father stepped toward the cubs. "It's almost time for lunch. Since all of you appear to be getting along, for the most part, let's go ahead and pull our chairs up to the table," Mr. Snow addressed the gang. "I'll ready the kitchen. They should be back down here in just a moment."

However, upstairs, things were not as smooth as Mr. Snow had hoped. Flurry continued to bawl his little eyes out. Mrs. Snow came into the room and found her boy lying on his bed. "Sweetie, it's all right. Don't cry, my son," Mrs. Snow consoled her teary-eyed cub.

Flurry's steady stream of tears resumed. He would not allow himself to be comforted. He sobbed throughout his reply. "I thought you loved me, but you replaced me!" Flurry bellowed before he returned to his sorrows. The cub buried his face in the tear-soaked pillow from his bed.

"We didn't replace you, Sweetie. Nothing could ever take your place. I've missed you more than you can imagine, and not a day has gone by where I haven't missed you dearly. But without you here, the home has been so ... empty. Your absence has left a hole in my heart that only you can fill. Fall was brought to us by Mr. Kringle, as a surprise gift. He thought she would help ease our pain. I thought you'd be happy to know that you have a sister. Think of the fun the two of you could have together."

"Whatever!"

"Don't be so selfish!" Flurry's mama gave him a lecture about his attitude, and attempted to explain more of how Fall came to be a part of their family.

Flurry sat up, rubbed his eyes, and then sat there in silence with a scowl upon his face.

"Wipe that look off of your mug right now!" Flurry's mama sharply rebuked him. "Flurry, I came here to comfort you, but if you're going to be difficult, you can just sit here in your room and think about it while the rest of us eat our lunch! It isn't fair to keep your guests waiting to eat just because you want to throw a pity party for yourself! You have a sister! Now, deal with it!" Mrs. Snow got up and stormed out of Flurry's room. Flurry did not react, but continued with his grumpy countenance. Eventually, he crawled under the blanket and hid there, as if it would effectively hide him from the rest of the world.

Mrs. Snow came downstairs and rejoined the rest of the guests at the table. "Well?" Mr. Snow asked, "How is he?"

"He's …" Mrs. Snow began and then paused when she changed her mind about what she was going to say. She rested her face in her paws momentarily and then looked up to reply, "He's being difficult. He has this crazy idea that we don't love him, and that we tried to replace him with Fall."

Mr. Snow sighed and rubbed the side of his face with his paw. Caboose looked over toward the steps, slid down from his chair, crawled under the table, and slipped away from the others, while Flurry's parents continued to converse about their son.

Nobody noticed Caboose's sly departure, as they all listened intently to the Snow family discussion.

Caboose had a bit of trouble getting up the steps, but he managed to climb them all and find Flurry's room, after a little exploration. Caboose came into the room, took ahold of the blanket with his mouth, and pulled the bedspread down to the floor.

Flurry looked up with his watery eyes and was relieved to see that it was Caboose. "Oh, hey, Caboose!" Flurry responded to his visitor.

"Hello," said Caboose.

"What are you doing here? I thought Mama was fixing lunch."

"Yes, she is, but you're my friend and friends stick togesser," Caboose answered, and climbed up on the bed and laid there with Flurry.

"I don't want to be here anymore! I wish we could sneak out without anyone noticing," Flurry replied, as he looked out from the window. After a momentary pause, Flurry thought of a plan, and his mood changed. He quickly cheered up as if a light bulb had turned on inside of his mind, giving him new insight and inspiration. "I know! We could go visit my uncle! His name is Vinegar. I could tell Mama and Papa that he wanted to see me. They'll believe me, and then we can use that as our excuse to get out of the house. Come on Caboose!"

"Lying is bad," Caboose answered.

"Okay. I won't lie to them. I'll think of something else," Flurry assured the little polar bear. "Maybe we can just sneak out instead."

Flurry and Caboose alighted from the bed and traversed the hallway in a furtive manner. Step-by-step, Flurry tiptoed down the length of the stairs and peeked out toward the guests gathered at the table. They were unaware of his presence. Flurry turned back to his friend atop of the steps and motioned with his paw for Caboose to follow.

Caboose, however, was not as careful as Flurry. He tromped along, without even attempting to be stealthy.

"Shhhhh!" Flurry exclaimed.

"Oh! Sorry!" Caboose replied, but at his usual volume level.

"Shhhhh! Caboose! You have to whisper!" Flurry shouted to the best of his ability while still trying to employ a whispery tone.

Caboose nodded and continued to descend the staircase. After only a couple of steps, he lost his footing and down he went. The polar bear tumbled, head over paw, the entire flight. Caboose grunted as he impacted each step. The poor cub landed on his belly with all four of his limbs splayed out at his side as though he were a polar bear rug on the polished hardwood floor.

Caboose sat up and rubbed his head. "Ouch!" he loudly exclaimed.

Flurry slapped his paw against his face in

disbelief. "Caboose! Now you blew our cover!" Flurry shouted back in frustration. Yet, to his surprise, nobody else reacted. It was as if the others had not noticed a thing. They were still at the table conversing while Flurry's mama cooked a meal. Flurry wondered how the others did not hear them. The trip from Flurry's bedroom was so loud that he worried that the neighbors could have heard it.

"Caboose, are you seeing this?" Flurry asked his companion.

"Uh huh! Say have food!" Caboose answered with his cute lisp.

"No! Not that!" Flurry shot back. "They don't seem to notice us at all! How can this be?"

It was possible because of that remaining miraculous power that resided within Flurry, but he still knew nothing about its presence. If he had known of this fact, he would have realized that he was the one that wished they could sneak out unnoticed. Flurry got his wish. It was as if he and Caboose were now invisible.

As most kids would do, Flurry had to push his luck and see how far he could take it. He waved his arms, jumped up and down, then hollered at them, but to no avail. It was as if Flurry and Caboose were not even there.

"This is really weird," Flurry concluded. "I've never seen this happen ..." Before he finished his thought, he quickly dismissed it all and was back on task. "Oh, well! Let's go, Caboose!"

They both made a beeline for the door. Flurry opened the door, allowed Caboose out first, and then followed after his friend. Flurry took in a deep breath of the crisp, cold air and shut the door behind them.

Now, even though Flurry and Caboose were able to get out unnoticed, it did not mean that the others did not see the door open and close. In fact, it seemed as though the door had operated all by itself. Mr. Snow got up and went to the entryway to investigate. He opened the door again but found nothing.

Fall watched from the table and noticed footprints in the snow that led away from the threshold. Without any explanation to anyone, Fall jumped out of her seat and ran to the open door.

She scanned the snow and saw new tracks being made right before her eyes. Fall could not believe what she was seeing. The young cub knew she had to investigate this. She called out to her parents, "I'll be right back!" and out of the house she scurried.

Mr. and Mrs. Snow turned to each other with perplexed looks on their faces. "Why is everyone acting so strangely today?" Mrs. Snow asked her husband.

Mr. Snow shrugged, looked out from the window, and saw Fall go around the corner and out of sight. "It would seem that she's more like her brother than we thought."

Mrs. Snow then turned her attention to her guests. "I'm so sorry for all of this. I don't know what has gotten into either of my cubs today."

"It's okay. We're used to it," Boaz answered. "Flurry is like this all the time. Right, Caboose? Caboose?"

Boaz's question was met with silence. He

and the others looked around for the polar bear's whereabouts. "Caboose!" Boaz called out.

By this point, Flurry and Caboose were quickly on their way to Flurry's uncle's study. They ran up to the door. Flurry rapped at the frigid oak barrier between them and a warm, private library. The sound of footsteps approached, followed by an inconvenienced voice. "Who is it?"

"It's me, Uncle!" Flurry replied.

"Me, who? Don't you have a name?" the voice shot back.

"Your favorite nephew, Flurry!"

There was a long pause before the voice muttered, "Why me? Can't I have a moment of peace?" The male inside then replied, "Go away! I don't have time for cubs!"

"Please?" Flurry beckoned.

"No!"

Flurry and Caboose sat in the snow and wondered what to do. Flurry then decided to knock again, but there was no answer. "Fine! I'm going to keep knocking until you open the door!" At that moment, Flurry got busy knocking.

The door burst open in haste. An elderly-looking teddy bear with gray fur and a wooden cane stood before them. His fur looked worn from many years of use. Flurry always assumed that it was because his Uncle was well-loved and likely received many hugs over the years. The elderly bear looked down at Flurry who had not stopped knocking, despite the door no longer being within his reach. "Would you stop it? You're driving me crazy!" the grumpy bear shouted. "This must be a record for you! It only took you two seconds!"

Flurry giggled, ran up, and hugged his uncle's leg. "Uncle Vinegar! I missed you!"

"Yes, yes, that's great. Now, what do you want? I have important work to do."

"Nothing."

"Nothing? Then why are you wasting my time?"

"I wanted to show Caboose your study. Can we look around?"

"No! Absolutely not!"

"Please?" Flurry looked up at his uncle with the cutest little eyes.

Vinegar sighed and gave in. "Oh, all right, but only for a few minutes, and then you two have to go back home. I'm sure my brother is wondering where you are."

"Yay! Thank you, Uncle!" Flurry and Caboose quickly entered the building.

Vinegar closed and latched the door behind them.

"Now, if you'll excuse me, I was in the middle of something important."

He paused a moment to mutter to himself, "Unlike entertaining you two," then continued with his ordinances. "You may look around, but don't touch anything!" Vinegar sternly ordered as he bent down and peered at Flurry through his spectacles.

"Of course, Uncle. Don't worry! You can always count on me!" Flurry tried to assure his uncle.

"Uh huh, that's what I'm afraid of," Vinegar murmured with a hint of sarcasm to his statement.

Vinegar's fur was completely gray with the exception of his snout, chin fur, and his bushy eyebrows, all of which were white.

His cane looked like a twisted tree branch, and despite the need for one, he was close to the same height as Flurry's papa. Flurry was too young to gauge the exact height in feet or inches. However, Flurry did recall that his papa stood as high as the light switches at his mother's house, when Mr. and Mrs. Snow had come to visit him in Middleasia.

Like Flurry, Vinegar, too, had a blue scarf wrapped around his neck with snowflakes at one end. These snowflakes were the trademark of the Snow family. Despite being the brother of Flurry's papa, Vinegar looked like he could easily be more than ten years older than Mr. Snow. In fact, Flurry thought it looked like there could be at least a ten year gap between all three siblings. Flurry's father was the middle brother.

Vinegar began to walk away, but then

turned to ask, "So who's that fella you have with you?"

"Oh! That's my friend, Caboose," Flurry replied.

Vinegar whispered under his breath as he commenced with the work he had piled up on his desk which sat in the northeastern corner of the study. Without even looking up from his work, Vinegar adjusted his reading glasses and asked, "Isn't a 'caboose' the last car of a train? How did he get a name like that?"

"My mommy named him … oops, I mean my new mommy, in Middleasia."

Vinegar did not reply, but that did not bother Flurry, because his focus had shifted to something more pressing. Caboose was now missing, and Flurry had no idea where he had gone. Flurry looked all around but could not find Caboose anywhere. He quickly looked under the furniture and behind the bookshelves in a frenzy. Flurry worried that Caboose might get them into trouble.

Flurry went up and down the small corridors created by Vinegar's stacks of old books and maps. Vinegar had an extensive collection that could almost rival a library. Well-known as a historian and archaeologist many years ago, he was an avid record keeper, and his map collection came from his love of cartography. Some of the maps he had collected on his own, while others were acquired through his youngest brother's adventures.

Vinegar loved to read rather than having to be around others. He much preferred to stay cooped up in his study with his nose buried in a book. A day between the pages of a good book was a day well spent, in Vinegar's opinion.

Flurry scanned the maze of literature. He knew that Caboose could be anywhere, and Flurry did not have any idea where else to start. Flurry did not even notice Caboose slip away.

Flurry panicked and was about to lose hope when he finally spotted Caboose near Vinegar's desk. *How did he get all the way over there?* Flurry thought to himself.

Flurry gasped when he saw what was about to transpire. Caboose tugged on one of the maps in the middle of a large stack of documents. Flurry knew where this was going to lead, and with a horrified look on his face, Flurry waved his arms back and forth and screamed, "No! Caboose! No!"

It was too late. The stack of maps crashed down on top of and around Caboose. Before anyone could even say "oops," Vinegar stood over Caboose with his paws firmly planted upon his hips. Vinegar looked exceptionally angry, so much so that Flurry expected to see steam come out from his uncle's ears. "What are you doing? I told you two not to touch anything! This is the opposite of not touching anything! You haven't even been in here for five minutes, and you've already made a mess! Get out! Both of you! Out, now!"

Vinegar grabbed Caboose by the fur on the back of his neck, carried him to the door, and tossed him out into a snow drift. He then looked back inside at Flurry and motioned with his paw for Flurry to get out, too. Flurry's head drooped as he slowly shuffled out the door. Flurry turned back and began, "I'm so …," but the door slammed shut and latched before Flurry could finish his sentence. "… sorry?"

Flurry beat on the door. "Uncle! Uncle! I'm sorry! Uncle?" Flurry waited for a moment, but he did not receive an answer. "Let's go, Caboose, I guess he isn't going to let us back in. Time to go home."

Caboose nodded his head, shook off the excess snow from his fur, and followed Flurry back up the path to reunite with their friends back at the house.

CHAPTER 3
CABOOSE'S MAP

Flurry and Caboose trekked up the hill in the direction of Flurry's home when they were met halfway. Their journey was obstructed by none other than Flurry's sister. She awaited their approach with her paws at her hips. Before Flurry could even react, Fall authoritatively asked, "And what do you think you're doing?"

Flurry's quick wits kicked in as he shot a glance at Caboose and bellowed, "Yeah, Caboose! What are you doing?"

"I'm not talking to him!" Fall snapped back. "I'm talking to you, Flurry!"

"Oh!" Flurry's mind raced as he tried to think of an adequate excuse. "You see … Caboose needs his ecersize so I went with him so he wouldn't get lost."

Though Fall was tempted to correct her brother's mispronunciation of "exercise", she simply responded with, "Oh, really?"

"Yep! Uh huh! Yeah, that's right!" Flurry grinned uneasily as he stood with his arms behind his back in his feeble attempt to look innocent.

"If that's so, then what were you doing at Uncle Vinegar's study?"

"Studying!"

"Studying for what?"

Flurry stumbled over his words in his scramble to try and find the best answer.

"Uh … we had to study how to ecersize the right way. You don't want to pull a muscle."

"You don't have any muscles! You're a teddy bear! Flurry, stop lying!"

"Caboose did it!" blurted from Flurry's mouth while he simultaneously raced past his sister at top speed. "Come on, Caboose! Run!"

Caboose and Flurry frantically dashed up the path to escape Fall's interrogation, but she chased after them. "Stop avoiding me, Flurry!" she shouted, but her brother did not respond. Flurry moved as diligently as his little legs would take him. Fall darted out ahead of him and with an outstretched arm, she hollered, "Stop! If you go any further, I'm going to tell Mama and Papa on you!"

Flurry froze in place. Caboose did not expect such a sudden halt and crashed right into Flurry, which toppled them both to the ground. When they stood back up to dust off the snow, Fall noticed something stuck to Caboose's backside.

"What's that?" Fall asked.

"What's what?" Flurry answered.

"That!"

"What?"

Fall did not have the patience to argue with her brother, so she marched over to Caboose and pulled a large piece of paper from his hindquarters. "It looks like a map," Fall said as she examined it.

Flurry quickly snatched it from her paws. "Give me that! It's ours! Or at least I think it's ours." After a brief inspection of the parchment, Flurry was not as sure of his previous statement. "Caboose, where did you get this?" Caboose shrugged in response. Flurry had a sinking feeling in his chest. "Uh oh! This might be one of Uncle Vinegar's maps!" A look of terror took hold of the cub.

"Maybe it got stuck to you when you knocked the pile of maps down. We should take this back right away, before Uncle Vinegar notices that it's missing. Hurry!"

Flurry sprinted back down the hill, but he was hindered by his sister's voice. "Stop! Don't you want to see what it is first?"

Flurry halted his departure and thought about it. He was certainly curious, but he also did not want to agree with his sister. He pondered how he could agree without looking like he was complying with her. "No, that's okay. We should take it back, unless Caboose wants to look at it."

Flurry turned his gaze toward Caboose

and winked. He expected, or at the very least hoped, that Caboose would play along and agree to look at it. Flurry should have known better. It was inevitable that Flurry would get upset when Caboose answered, "Huh?"

"You know, the map. Did you want to look at it before I take it back to Uncle Vinegar?"

"No, sank you," Caboose replied.

"Here!" Fall exclaimed, as she ripped the map from Flurry's paws. Fall opened the faded document. Her face looked intrigued. "Wow! Look at this, Flurry!"

Flurry stood there with his arms crossed, unwilling to budge.

"Fine! Suit yourself! I'm going to go there on my own, and all of the goodies will be mine!" she taunted.

"What goodies?" Fall now had Flurry's full attention. "Let me see that!" he shouted as he snagged the map back from his sister. "Ooh! It's a map to the land of sour pies." Flurry still could not read, but he knew the word "sour" and the word "pie" from the package labels at his mother's house.

"No silly! It's the land of the Sourpie," Fall corrected.

"So what? Same difference!"

"No, it's not! For starters, it's one word, not to mention that the 's' is capitalized. It looks more like a proper noun than a food."

"Whatever that means! You're starting to sound like Drizzle! What's important is that they have pie. If they have sour pies, they likely have sweet pies, too. I bet they have all kinds of pies. It's a land full of pie! Yum! Yum!" Flurry grew even more excited.

"Flurry! I was kidding, just to get you to look at the map! There aren't really any goodies!"

"Sure! You say that now!" Flurry's distrust was easily deduced.

Fall grunted in frustration. "I can't believe you're my brother!" Fall shouted right before she sighed, plopped down on the cobblestone path, and pouted.

"I know. I am pretty awesome!" Flurry giggled, but Fall was not amused. "Come on, Caboose! Let's go get some pie!"

"Wait a minute!" Fall was swiftly back to her feet and stood in Flurry's path once again. "You can't just leave! Mama and Papa will be wondering where you are."

"They won't even notice. They don't care about me. It's clear that they love you more," Flurry passionately replied while he fought back tears.

"Flurry! You can be such a brat! That's not true! Mama and Papa love both of us equally!"

"Nice try! You aren't fooling me!" Flurry turned and began back down the path; in the direction the map seemed to be pointing him. Caboose followed closely behind while Fall trailed at a distance. She continued her attempt to talk Flurry out of his foolish idea.

"Flurry! What if something bad happens? What if you get hurt or lost? Shouldn't you tell Mama and Papa where you're going?"

When it was clear that she was being ignored, she shouted, "Stop, right this instant! I'm going to tell on you!" Fall had tried everything she could think of, but Flurry discounted her every word. The boys traipsed out of the village and beyond the great arch that stood as a landmark and gateway at the edge of the southern border to and from the land of Mezarim. After a number of hours they were about to venture beyond Christopher Kringle's territory.

More time had passed, and they were now continuing on without a path. The snow was deeper, and the wind was colder and stronger.

"Flurry! I really think we should head back now!" Fear was in Fall's voice as she tried to speak up over the strong wind that blew steadily upon them.

Without warning, the wind plucked the map from Flurry's paws and sent it soaring out ahead of them.

"Hurry! We have to catch the map!" Flurry shouted and darted after it. Caboose and Fall chased after their brash companion.

They were in hot pursuit of the map, but the wind continued to blow it just out of their reach. The cubs were uncertain how long they had sought after the map, but they eventually reached the edge of a pine forest where they stopped to catch their breath. One thing was for certain, they were a long way from home.

They had traveled far enough that grass appeared more and more frequently. The snow was now so sparse that it looked like it had fallen in small, isolated patches on top of the green turf beneath their feet. The orange clouds evoked concern when Fall realized how low the sun had sunk toward the horizon.

"Flurry, we're never going to catch that map. This is all your fault! We should go home and confess to Uncle Vinegar that we lost his map!" Fall snapped at her brother.

"Well, nobody asked you to come along!" Flurry shot back.

The siblings argued, but Caboose had his sights still set on the prize. Among the branches of a towering cedar, Caboose spotted the map. Without hesitation, he set forth to scale the tree and apprehend his prize. While Flurry and Fall continued their feud, Caboose's exit went unnoticed.

Their bickering continued to get more and more heated. They name called and pushed each other. Then there was abrupt silence. The siblings stood motionless, as if they had turned to stone. Flurry cautiously inquired, "Uh … where's Caboose?"

"I don't know. He was right here a second ago," Fall answered.

"Okay, but he's not here now." Flurry

looked around and called out to his friend, "Caboose! Caboose! Where are you?"

The two bear cubs traveled deeper into the woods, ceaselessly calling out to their missing friend. Fear and concern consumed them both. They were relieved to finally hear a small, faint voice which answered, "Up here! I'm up here!"

"That sounded like Caboose, but I don't see him," Flurry mentioned to his sister.

"Look! Up there!" Fall pointed at the branches of a nearby tree.

"Oh, my! Caboose! What are you doing up there?" Flurry worried for his friend's safety.

"Oh, it's nussing. I just found suh map." As he said this, the branch broke and Caboose tumbled down the tree. The poor cub hit each successive branch as he plummeted into a pile of pine needles. Caboose looked up, embarrassed, just as the map gracefully glided down and landed on top of his head.

Overjoyed, both Flurry and Fall ran to Caboose and hugged him while they unanimously shouted, "You did it!" Caboose sat among the pine needles and blushed.

Flurry did not waste any time before he reasserted himself as the leader. He promptly grabbed the map and continued. "Okay! Now, it looks like we're here at the 'pine forest', as the map says." Flurry deduced this based on the little drawings of trees and not on his ability to read the text. "We need to go to this grassy spot on the map. Let's go!" Without hesitation, Flurry hurried away.

Fall helped Caboose up and brushed him

off. "Come on, Caboose, we can't let Flurry have all of the glory."

Caboose and Fall trailed close behind Flurry as he led them out of one wilderness and into another just beyond the set of small hills. This territory had a variety of trees that looked different than any Fall had ever seen before.

All of the cubs took account of the more menacing look their new environment presented. The foliage was thicker, and the foreboding trees grew all the more sinister as the sun inched its way closer to the horizon. Darkness hastily embraced the land, as if it were choking out the light from every direction.

"Uh, Flurry? Shouldn't we be heading back now? It's getting dark." Fall had deep concern in her voice.

"Don't be silly! We're only getting started. How will we ever reach the tasty pies if we stop now?"

"But Flurry! We've already been gone way too long! Mama and Papa are probably worried sick about us!" Fall pleaded.

"Worried sick about you, maybe! They probably don't know I'm even gone." A tear slid down Flurry's cheek.

"Flurry! I told you that's not true! Quit being so selfish! You aren't the center of the world!"

"Well, maybe I should be!" Flurry wittingly replied.

"Well, I don't care what you think. We need to go back home!" It was evident that her reply was ignored. Fall did not know what else to do. They had all made rather poor decisions that day, and she was concerned that the consequences for their actions were closer than she would like them to be.

Fall whined, "I'm cold, it's getting dark, and we don't have any food." Seeing that she received nothing but silence, Fall tried to reason with her brother. "We don't even have a flashlight! How are we going to find our way in the dark anyway?"

"Of course! Just like a girl to want to chicken out!"

Flurry's harsh words wounded Fall deeply. Fall wept, "Flurry! You're so mean! Why do you have to be like that?"

Fall ran off a short distance from her brother and cried. She buried her face in her paws in an attempt to hide her tears. Caboose strolled up to her and laid his head on her lap, much like a faithful and loving puppy would do. She patted him on the head and whispered, "Caboose, you're such a good bear. If only Flurry could be more like you."

Flurry sat by himself and debated about what he should do. He looked over his shoulder and saw Fall as she sat on a log with his faithful friend. Initially he felt angry, and he thought to himself, *She's ruining everything! First she steals my parents away from me, and now she steals my friends, too!* However, his anger quickly faded to make way for the guilt which now crept into his heart. Flurry felt remorse for the way he had treated his sister.

Flurry got up and walked over to join them. "I'm sorry for being mean to you. I didn't mean to say those things, and I didn't mean to hurt you. I was just angry." Flurry looked up at Fall to find his gaze met with a smile while she wiped away her tears.

"I forgive you," Fall replied as she opened her arms for a hug.

"I said I'm sorry, but I don't think I need a hug." Flurry's words were met with a frown. With a sigh, he consented. "Oh, okay."

"Yay!" Fall exclaimed as she clutched Flurry tightly.

Without a moment of hesitation, Flurry pushed her away, straightened his scarf, cleared his throat, and said, "That's enough! Okay, we should find a good spot to sleep tonight. We can continue in the morning." All of them agreed to this and decided to venture only a little further in search of an adequate resting spot.

They had not progressed very far before

they heard a loud snap. "What was that?" Fall nervously asked.

"Oh, it was probably nothing," Flurry tried to assure her.

Then another loud snap echoed through the wooded landscape. "Did you hear that?" The concern in Fall's voice was even more apparent.

"It was probably just a little squirrel or something like that." Flurry tried to relieve her uneasiness, but even he felt spooked.

The wind rustled the leaves, crickets chirped, and an owl hooted from a distance. It might have seemed like any other eerie forest, but a menacing growl took their dread to a new level. Fall insisted on what she knew to be a growl, but Flurry remained skeptical. He did not want to believe that they were in grave danger, though he too had heard the same thing.

Then it came again. A loud snap, followed by another, and then another. The snaps were accompanied by growling. The cubs shook in terror. It was clear that they were being followed by something that was out there in the darkness with them. Nightfall's progression quickly made the forest creepier by the minute, and Flurry did not have a light source available to illuminate their path.

"Flurry! Please tell me you hear that! Don't tell me it's nothing!" Fall's voice was saturated with dread.

"Uh …" Flurry began, and his tone clearly conveyed that he was just as spooked as his sister. "I hear it. Let's all stand close together, and we should be fine." After Flurry's attempt to bolster some courage,

Fall wrapped her arms around her brother's. Flurry glanced at the ground with a bewildered look upon his face. Caboose was missing. "Wait a minute! Where's Caboose?" Flurry inquired.

"Oh no! Not again! I hope he didn't get eaten by whatever it is making those sounds," Fall answered.

"Caboose?" Flurry attempted to call out, but his voice trembled with trepidation. Instead, Caboose's name came forth from Flurry's mouth at the level of a whisper. "Caboose?"

"Hello!" shouted a voice from the darkness.

"Ahhh!" Flurry and Fall screamed while they clenched each other tightly.

"It's just me! Caboose! Look what I found! A friend!" Caboose stood next to what appeared to be a wolf. The beast had sharp teeth, yellow eyes, and gray fur. However, there were details about this wolf that made it clear that this was not an ordinary one. The wolf stood taller than most and had light blue markings all over its fur. It also had an earring in each ear and decorative armor plates just above the paws. Caboose continued with his introduction. "She's very nice. Say hello."

The wolf opened its mouth and spoke. "You aren't safe here!" A female voice came forth from the wolf's maw. "You may be safe from me, but this forest is extremely dangerous. There are many beasts that would rip you to shreds."

"So you aren't going to eat us?" Flurry inquired cautiously.

"I had hoped that the three of you were

going to be my dinner, but you aren't real bears at all. You are of no nutritional value to anyone." Flurry let out a resounding sigh of relief.

"So you really aren't going to eat us?" Flurry hesitantly asked again. He needed to be sure he had heard her correctly.

"Of course not! You're nothing but fur and stuffing. I long for meat."

Fall let out a sigh of her own and let go of Flurry's arm. The young cub approached the wolf and asked, "What's your name?"

"My name isn't important," the wolf replied.

"Well, my name is Fall. This is my brother, Flurry, and you've already met Caboose."

The wolf groaned and then relented. "My pack calls me Wolfhroc. I'm a warrior among my kin. In fact, I'm the best scout in the land of Canidore. There are a number of different wolf packs. I'm from Pack Isangrim, named after our noble and fearless leader."

"It's an honor to meet you, Wolfhroc," Fall continued. "I'm so sorry to bother you about this, but can you help us find a safe place to sleep?"

"My pack is a long way from here. I go out scouting well ahead of the rest. It would take too long to bring you to them tonight. That's the only way you would truly be safe out here in the wild. Being alone in this forest you'll be vulnerable and make for easy prey."

"Can't you help us?" Fall pleaded.

"I'm sorry, but I must continue hunting for food. The best of luck to all of you."

Before she could walk away, Flurry had something to add. "Well, before you go, can you tell me if we're on the right path?" Flurry opened up the map and showed it to the wolf.

The wolf's eyes widened. Flurry had her full attention. "Where did you get this?" asked the wolf.

"From my uncle. Why?"

"This map leads to a forbidden land. You mustn't go there!" she gravely warned.

"Why? What's wrong with it?"

"There's a rumor that the inhabitants of that land had a feud which caused their nation to split in two. One group became very prosperous and continues to live on a nearby island. The other group, however, are said to be cursed. These are probably nothing more than stories, but it's believed that anyone who enters that land will share in their curse. My kind avoids that region at all costs."

"It can't be that bad! They have pie!" Flurry responded.

"Foolish little one! The map doesn't speak of a land of pies! It's the land of the Sourpie! It's ruled by King Sourpuss himself!"

"Yeah, that's what I said; sour pie, but surely they have other pies. Better yet, maybe they don't just have pies. Maybe they have lots of other tasty treats, too."

"You just don't get it. What I'm saying is …" Wolfhroc paused when she observed Flurry licking his lips. It was clear that he was not listening her. "Never mind. I tell you what, I'll stay with you tonight, and tomorrow you can come with me and meet the rest of my family."

"Wow! That sounds great!" Flurry enthusiastically replied.

"Good! It's settled then. Let's gather up some wood and build a fire. We shall sleep here tonight."

All of them picked up branches and brought them to the wolf while she built them a fire. As the cubs gathered firewood, Flurry approached his sister. "This is going to be so great! See! I told you! We have nothing to worry about!" Fall gave an uneasy grin in response, for she did not share in Flurry's optimism.

Meanwhile, back in Ursus, things were not going well at all. Despite the sun still being up, evening had come and the entire teddy bear community had been out scouring the town the entire day. They continued to search for the missing bear cubs. Mr. and Mrs. Snow were a complete wreck. Mrs. Snow had been crying so much that her dress had become soaked with tears that were now ice. Mr. Snow put on a brave face for his wife and helped with the search. They could not understand where their cubs had disappeared to.

Mrs. Snow blamed herself. "This wouldn't have happened if I hadn't been so firm with Flurry. He was really hurt. I hope he didn't do anything foolish, like running away," she relayed to her husband. Mr. Snow put his arm around her and wiped away her tears with his other paw.

Flurry's friends contributed to the search. Even Flurry's Uncle Vinegar partook in the hunt. Vinegar had explained to his brother that he had yelled at Flurry and threw him out of his study. Vinegar felt responsible for Flurry and Fall's disappearance just as much as Mr. and Mrs. Snow did.

Despite the seemingly dire circumstances, Mr. Kringle had a feeling that Flurry, Fall, and Caboose were okay. Christopher had concealed from everyone secret knowledge he harbored in the back of his mind for many years. The tall, bearded man had an inkling about the bear, and he was patient enough to wait and see if his hunch be true.

Knowing Flurry's adventurous spirit, and after he heard from Vinegar that a map was missing, Christopher deduced that the cubs were probably following whichever map they had found. However, Christopher did not want to bring this up with Mr. and Mrs. Snow quite yet. He did not want to give them false hope, nor did he want the same information to make them worry, either, depending on how they would react to the news.

Despite wherever Flurry might be, Christopher had confidence in Flurry's resilience, and he knew that Flurry would make it back to them in one piece.

CHAPTER 4
THE JOURNEY

Flurry and his companions woke early, just as the sun ascended from the horizon. Wolfhroc had been awake long before the rest of them. Flurry opened his eyes to find the wolf pacing to and fro, as if she had protected them all throughout the night. "Good! You're up!" exclaimed Wolfhroc. "We need to get moving if we're to catch up with the rest of my pack. I'm sure they've begun journeying south already. Since that's your destination as well, you may come with us. You'll be our guests."

"Wow! That sounds great!" Flurry shouted with excitement.

"Uh … Flurry? How can we possibly keep up with her?" Fall asked her brother.

Before Flurry could think of a reply, Wolfhroc answered for him. "All of you may ride on my back. The three of you are exceptionally light." The gray wolf crouched low to the ground to allow for the cubs to embark. "Quickly, we mustn't waste any more time."

Their new friend was swift on her feet. Flurry and his companions had mounted the wolf only seconds before Wolfhroc launched herself across the wooded terrain. The she wolf gracefully and briskly dashed through the branches and bushes. Flurry was filled with excitement as he watched the trees become nothing but a blur while they rapidly moved from one location to the next. This was the most fun Flurry had ever experienced.

As they traversed large portions of land, Flurry and the others took in the scenic view. They first crossed a beautiful green meadow where the grass stood almost as tall as Flurry. After the meadow came a river of crystal clear water which rolled over smooth, polished stones that displayed a green hue of quartz.

They eventually ran into another wooded region along their path. This one was more open than the previous forests they had passed through. Here the ground was covered with delightful yellow flowers as far as the eye could see. Upon withdrawing from the last woodland, they came to a cliff that overlooked a large valley. The gorge below had a winding river that passed through the center flanked on each bank by blossoming trees. From the precipice, large mountains could be seen in the distance with caps of snow on each of them.

"Within that mountain range you'll find the land of the Sourpie. Our journey together ends once we reach the valley below," Wolfhroc told her riders.

Just as she spoke, howls could be heard in the distance. Wolfhroc replied with a loud call of her own. Flurry uncovered his ears when Wolfhroc spoke again. "That's my pack down below. We're almost there. Hold on, we must make our descent."

Flurry, Fall, and Caboose clasped tightly to the wolf's fur. Without delay, Wolfhroc descended the steep side of the bluff while

Flurry and his comrades tried to maintain their grip. They each held as tightly as they possibly could. Wolfhroc had amazing control and balance. She moved with such grace that traversing the side of the cliff looked like a walk in the park for her.

At last they reached the valley filled with all of the cherry blossom trees that the cubs had gazed upon from the peak above. Wolfhroc traipsed through seemingly endless curtains of grass that stood well above all of their heads. However, this was not a deterrent for the wolf; her nose had already picked up the scent of her kin.

It was not long until they reached a clearing where Flurry, Fall, and Caboose disembarked. However, Flurry was not sure that their venture was such a good idea any longer. He began to have second thoughts when they found themselves surrounded by other wolves that growled and bared their teeth at the young cubs.

"It's okay! They're with me!" Wolfhroc informed them with her authoritative tone.

As Wolfhroc spoke, an enormous canine emerged from the foliage behind the other wolves. This wolf had more of an imposing presence than all of the others. This beast looked dignified, commanding, and strong. He wore iron plates upon his head that cascaded over the crown of his head right down to his snout. The armor had decorative markings all across its surface with various nicks and scratches that conveyed extensive use or battle damage. The artwork on the armor had three ornate wolves in the midst of knotwork and spirals.

His neck was adorned with a stone

necklace held together by red chords. At the center of this elegant piece sat a large, crimson gemstone. The ornament looked much like something from the ancient Mayan culture Flurry had learned about from his mother in Middleasia.

The wolf was also marked upon his fur, just above each leg. These designs were of a different tint of gray than the rest of his coat. It appeared as though his fur had been bleached purposely to create such patterns. The other wolves had similar designs, but theirs were darker than their natural fur color.

It was clear that this was the leader of the pack. His voice was deep, and his words resounded when he spoke, much like the aftershocks of striking a gong. It was uncertain to Flurry if the wolf spoke with sincerity or sarcasm when he replied to Wolfhroc's statement, "Well, in that case, a friend of yours is a friend of ours. Isn't that right, boys?"

When he glanced at the other wolves; they each smirked or chuckled. Some of them replied, "That's right! ... Friends!"

Fall pulled her brother aside to voice her concern. "Flurry, I have a bad feeling about this."

"What's there to worry about? They told us that they're our friends," Flurry responded.

"I don't think we should trust the word of strangers until they've proven they can be trusted. Especially not the word of a wolf."

Her speech fell on deaf ears as she watched Flurry rush up to the wolf. "Hello, I'm Flurry! What's your name?"

"Flurry, stop!" Fall shouted.

The wolves all turned their attention to Fall. "What's with her?" the leader asked.

"Who? Her? Oh, she's nobody. Don't mind her," Flurry answered.

"Nobody? Nobody? Flurry! I'm your sister!" Fall was furious with Flurry's unscrupulous behavior.

Flurry grinned uneasily at the wolf and continued. "Yeah, she keeps saying that. I think she might be a little crazy. I don't have a sister."

In an outrage, Fall shouted, "What?"

"Ha, ha, ha, ha, ha! Sibling rivalry! How cute! Don't worry, your secret is safe with me," the towering wolf replied with a wink. The wolf sat down and motioned with his paw for Flurry's presence. "Come here! I like you!" The wolf put his paw around

Flurry, and rubbed the cub's head as he laughed.

"Very well. If you must know, my name is Isangrim. I'm the leader of Pack Isangrim." Then, as he pointed to himself, he continued in a very smug tone, stating, "Obviously named after me." Isangrim turned his gaze at the other cubs and then back at Flurry. "Welcome, Flurry and … how shall I address the other two?"

"That's my friend, Caboose, and the 'other' one is named Fall," Flurry responded.

"The 'other' one? I'm not just an 'other', Flurry! I'm your sister!" Fall was even more enraged over Flurry's treatment of her.

"There now, no need to fight. We're all friends here. Wolfhroc, take the others to our camp. I want to have some time to talk with Flurry," Isangrim ordered.

"As you wish," Wolfhroc replied with a bow. She then escorted Fall and Caboose through the grass and on up to the pack's campsite amidst the cherry blossom trees that enveloped everything in sight throughout their valley.

"Now, tell me, what brings you all of the way down here? You're a long way from Christopher Kringle's protection."

Flurry began to ask, "How did ..."

"I know?" Isangrim completed Flurry's inquiry. With a chuckle Isangrim continued. "There's a lot I know, little bear. Where else would a living, breathing teddy bear come from, if not the land of Mezarim?"

Being surprised by this, Flurry asked, "So you know Santa then?"

"Santa?" There was a brief pause while

Isangrim contemplated Flurry's question. The wolf grinned and answered, "Is that what you call him? Ha, ha, ha, ha, ha! Yes! Yes! I know him! I mean, who doesn't?" As Isangrim said this he winked at the other wolves that stood nearby. Isangrim's subordinates laughed and snickered.

Isangrim continued. "However, wolves aren't allowed that far north. Christopher's … excuse me … I mean 'Santa's' elves make sure of that."

"But Mrs. Kringle has a wolf of her own. They let him be there. He's really nice!"

Upon hearing Flurry's reply, the other wolves were enraged. Isangrim acted quickly. He stood tall and raised his voice. "Calm down! Calm down! All of you, calm down!"

"But, sir! We wouldn't be in our current

situation if not for that traitorous beast!" one of the other wolves argued.

Questioning Isangrim was a detrimental mistake. Isangrim growled, quickly turned to the other wolf, grabbed him by the throat, and slammed his face into the sod. "I told you to let it go! This isn't the time or the place for that conversation!"

Flurry was concerned. He rushed up to stand between Isangrim and the humiliated wolf. "Maybe it's all just a mistake. You're so nice. I don't see why you wouldn't be welcome." Flurry was so sure of his own reasoning that the squabble he had just witnessed did not faze him at all. Nothing struck the cub as suspicious, though it should have.

Isangrim's gaze turned from his subordinate to the cub. "Well, not everyone is as understanding or as clever as you are."

Isangrim quickly steered the conversation back on track and continued. "However, we've digressed. What were we talking about? Oh yes! So, why are you down here?"

"Well, Caboose and I found this map to the land of sour pies. We're hoping they have other goodies there, too."

A smirk came to Isangrim's face. He looked over at the other wolves who chuckled in response. "Indeed they do, young one! However, there are far better goodies in the island city of Tikalico."

"Like what? Cookies? Cake? Ice cream?"

"Yes! Yes! I'm sure they do. However, nobody can enter that city; they have it well-protected. This protection prevents even their own brothers and sisters from entering."

"I can understand that," Flurry said with a nod of agreement.

"That's right! You know what it's like to have a sibling take what's rightfully yours, don't you?"

"Uh huh!" Flurry nodded again.

"The Tikalico nation was so rude to their own brothers and sisters that they split off from them and banished them to a forsaken land after giving them the name 'Sourpie'."

"Oh, so that's why their pie is sour," Flurry reasoned.

"Why, yes! Of course! Now you see!" Flurry nodded in agreement, and Isangrim continued. "It's such a wonderful thing that you've arrived. You could help the Sourpie and the others by your bravery and cunning." Flurry felt good about what he heard. He imagined himself as the hero that saved the sour pies from going to waste. Isangrim had a crooked grin on his face as he went on. "You see this necklace I wear around my neck?"

"Uh huh!"

"Well, this is one of two necklaces that I once possessed. I was going to give one to the Sourpie in order to break the curse, but their enemies from Tikalico stole it. If you could retrieve the necklace from Tikalico, it would finally make things right. Think of it, you could be the one to lift the curse from the Sourpie. They would be so grateful that they would probably make you their king and give you all of the tasty treats you can imagine."

Now, it would be clear to most individuals that Isangrim was up to no good.

However, he said the things that Flurry wanted to hear and that aided in his deception. Flurry imagined being king and no longer having a need for his parents' love or attention. As king, he could do anything he wanted. He could stay up late, eat nothing but sweets, and play games every day.

"Wow!" Flurry shouted. His ego had just been further inflated by Isangrim's words. The young cub now had even greater delusions of grandeur than what was typical of him.

While in the middle of his daydream, Flurry was abruptly interrupted. "Don't listen to him, Flurry! He's lying!" Fall shouted as she stormed out from the grass.

"What's this? You're our guests here, and you come out with baseless accusations against me?" Isangrim snapped at Fall.

Wolfhroc rushed out after the cub. The she wolf matched her gaze with Isangrim's and froze in her tracks. Wolfhroc cowered down. "I'm so sorry, master. She just ran off. I apologize for her intrusion. It won't happen again."

She picked Fall up with her mouth and carried her back through the grass, though Fall kicked and screamed the entire way. "No! Stop! Put me down! Don't listen to them, Flurry! Don't listen! They lie! Don't listen!"

As Fall's screams faded away in the distance, Isangrim turned back to Flurry, grinned, and then said, "Wow! I see what you mean. She really is crazy!"

"Yeah! At least you understand. Nobody else seems to believe me," Flurry replied.

"Oh, dear Flurry, I understand how you

feel all too well. However, to show that I'm really your friend, I shall help you reach the land of the Sourpie. It's very dangerous, and I'm putting my pack at risk, but it's the least I can do to show you that you can trust me. However, once we arrive, we shall need to part ways. It wouldn't be safe for my kind to enter that land."

Flurry nodded with approval. Isangrim stood up and strolled toward the little bear. "Let us go gather your friends and be on our way. Why put off until tomorrow what you can do today? If we move quickly, we can reach the mountains in a couple of days."

As Flurry ran off through the grass, Isangrim looked at the trio of wolves that stood close by. "You three! Journey on ahead of us. Scout out the land and lay low. Wait for our arrival." Without hesitation, the wolves took off through the grass. Then, Isangrim turned to the others, "As for the rest of you, be prepared. This could be the moment we've been waiting for after so many years. Stay alert and follow my lead."

Isangrim rushed off through the foliage to catch up with Flurry. "Flurry! My friend! Wait for me! I'm right behind you."

As Flurry and Isangrim arrived in the clearing where Fall, Caboose, and Wolfhroc sat, it was clear that Fall had been crying the entire time. She continued to sob and sniffle while she rubbed her eyes. Upon Flurry's appearance she ran up and hugged him. Tears streamed down her face as she pleaded with her brother, "Flurry, let's go home! I want to go home! I don't like it here! I miss Mama and Papa!"

Flurry was about to answer, but Isangrim

quickly stepped between them. "All right, let's go! Flurry, you may ride with me. You two, ride with Wolfhroc. Let's be off!"

"Huh? Wait a minute! What's going on?" Fall shouted.

"We're going to the land of sour pies, silly," Flurry answered.

Flurry climbed onto Isangrim's back while Isangrim lifted Caboose onto Wolfhroc. The female wolf did the same with Fall, regardless of the cub's wishes.

Fall was still determined to persuade her brother. "Flurry! Listen to me! You can't trust …" She was cut short when Isangrim ran off with Flurry on his back.

Before Fall had a moment to think, she, Caboose, and Flurry were all in transit upon the backs of wolves. The rest of the pack followed. She could not help but feel a sense of fear sweep over her. She worried for her brother's safety. Fall knew how easy it could be to stoke his ego, entice him with tasty treats, and make promises of glory. Though she had only just met her brother, her mama and papa had told her all about him, both his strengths and his weaknesses. If she were to get through to Flurry, she would need to come up with something that would rival anything that Isangrim might have offered or promised to her brother. Fall would have to tap Flurry's strengths if she were ever going to save him from this mess.

Flurry was not a bad bear; he really was not. The bear cub quite often meant well. He was not being mean to Fall for the sake of being cruel; he simply felt replaced and unloved, despite how ridiculous of a notion that was. Isangrim made Flurry feel wanted, needed, and valuable at just the right time – when Flurry was most vulnerable.

Fall contemplated how to get through to her brother, but she continued to come up empty-pawed. She had to think of something, but what? She did not want to lie. She had been taught that lying is wrong. A lot of thought would have to be put into this, but at least she had Caboose to keep her company while she plotted and planned a way to expose the wolves for what she knew them to be – predators.

CHAPTER 5
THE SOURPIE

After the long journey, one which took a number of days, the wolves, along with Flurry, Fall, and Caboose, arrived at the edge of a tree line. "This is where we part ways," Isangrim said to Flurry and the others. "Good luck with your mission."

"Thanks!" Yet, Flurry was uncertain what he was expected to do next. "What am I supposed to do again?" he asked.

"We're at the border of Sourpie territory. We don't venture into their land. You may go in, but we shall stay out. When you retrieve the necklace from the nation city of Tikalico, come to the edge of this forest and call my name. One of us shall be nearby at all times."

"Okay!" Flurry answered and waved goodbye to his wolf friends, as he, Fall, and Caboose entered the jungle together.

Now that Flurry was out of sight, Isangrim turned back to the others. "This is our moment! All of you, be ready! If he succeeds in getting that necklace, their defenses will be down and we'll have a feast. Be flexible. If he isn't successful in retrieving the necklace, his presence alone may still open a window of opportunity for us to exploit."

"Sir, if you don't mind me asking …" One of the subordinate wolves spoke up.

"Why can't we just make a meal out of the Sourpie now? They're quite exposed. These cats don't have a protected city like they do in Tikalico."

"Do you not know of the curse? Do you really want to partake in that curse with them? If so, then by all means, go make a meal out of them. I, however, have my sights set on greater things that don't involve coming under a curse." Isangrim snarled as he walked away from the other wolf.

Back in the jungle, Flurry struggled to push through the dense vegetation. This jungle was vastly different than the other forests they had been in before. Everything was damp, and the air felt moist and heavy. The vegetation was very thick, and Flurry could barely see beyond only a few feet ahead of him. The trees looked very different, with many of them not having branches low enough that he could grab ahold of and climb. At the tops of some of the trees were large brown spheres and in other trees were different types of fruits. Caboose spotted a number of banana trees along their path. The polar bear found every bit of their adventure fascinating.

The climate was very hot, and the water bubbled and steamed. They made certain to steer clear of the geysers they happened upon from time-to-time. Flurry had never been in such scorching heat before, and it was not a pleasant experience for him either. In fact, Flurry was quite astounded at how high the temperature was since he had not experienced geothermal activity before. The mountains that enclosed the region created a natural barrier from the outside world, which kept the cold out and trapped the heat in.

Darkness approached, and Flurry knew that they would soon need a light source. This time they were more prepared than before. The morning after their stay in the foreboding woods, Wolfhroc had given Flurry flint stones in order to make a fire. Little did Flurry realize how valuable of a skill she had imparted to him. "We should make a torch," Flurry informed the others. "It's getting dark, and we don't want to get lost."

Fall did not show any sign of having heard him. She was still immensely upset with her brother. During their time traveling with the wolves, Flurry spent most of the trip with Isangrim and ignored his sister.

Fall chose to remain silent and watch as her brother pulled out his flint stones and struck them over the branch he had fashioned into a torch. Within moments, the branch was ablaze with radiant, orange light. Flurry was quite pleased with his first torch. He lifted it above his head and continued to lead his party through the thick jungle as the darkness settled in all around them.

While they traversed the foliage, Flurry noticed stone structures in the distance. Some of the structures were very tall and towered above the trees while others were only slightly larger than Flurry himself. The further they traveled, the more the jungle opened up, and a path became clear to them.

When they drew near to the monolithic structures, they discovered statues and stone carvings in the rock face. Everything had a feline aesthetic to it. "Look!" Fall exclaimed, as she pointed to a magnificently large stone head with its mouth open. This rock structure was at least four times their height. If they had wanted to, they easily could have crawled up and into the open mouth of this decorative stone head. "It kind of looks like a cat, don't you think?" Fall asked.

Flurry did not have time to answer her because the rustling of leaves in the distance grabbed his attention. "Did you hear that?" Flurry asked.

"Yes, I did. I think something's coming," Fall answered.

Caboose quickly took cover behind Fall's legs. After all, he was sure that whatever rustled through the leaves would never find him behind Fall.

"I wonder what it is," Flurry commented to the other two. "Maybe the wolves came back?" Suddenly Flurry spun around and waved his torch back and forth.

"What's wrong?" Fall exclaimed with concern.

"Nothing. I just thought I heard a whisper."

"A whisper?"

"Yeah! Didn't you hear it?"

"No ..." Fall's reply was cut short when she too heard whispers come from the branches above them. "On second thought, yes. I did hear something that time."

"See! I'm not crazy! It sounds like whispering."

"Flurry, we're not alone anymore. I think I see something in the branches."

Flurry looked around and tried to adjust

his eyes to see if there was anything in the brush or on the branches. Flurry was about to shrug it off when he saw something move. "There!" Flurry shouted. "I saw something move. There it is again! There! There's another!" Flurry pointed to various trees. Caboose dropped lower to the ground and tried to hide himself under Fall's dress.

Suddenly, Flurry became specchless when the flame of his torch illuminated numerous sets of eyes that peered out at them from the flora. The bear cub could not find the words to articulate his thoughts, so his sister spoke on their behalf. "Uh, Flurry ... I think we have company ... and lots of it."

Fall grabbed Flurry's arm while Caboose cowered at her leg. The three of them were very frightened and huddled together for support. As they grasped tightly to each other, two dark figures came toward them. These two figures were about the same height as Flurry, which meant that they were far too small to be wolves.

The silhouetted forms continued to draw nearer and nearer from the jungle brush. The light from Flurry's torch revealed that they were cats, but they walked on their hind legs and held spears with their front paws. It was apparent to Fall that these cats were not ordinary house cats.

Each cat had stripes painted on their faces, and they wore jewelry that looked very similar to the necklace Isangrim wore. As Fall watched, many more cats emerged from the foliage. They, too, were covered in paint and jewelry. Many of them wore headdresses of some sort. Some of them carried bows while others carried spears. A few of them had knives and hatchets. All of the feline inhabitants looked grumpy and downright mean. Each cat had a different color of fur. Some of them were black while others were white, gray, brown, and even orange. A number of them had spots while others bore stripes. They were quite a diverse bunch of cats.

It became clear, very quickly, that these cats posed a danger to the young bear cubs. It was unknown if these felines were hostile or not, but Flurry had a hunch that they were. Flurry tried to muster up enough courage to speak with them, despite his fear of being attacked. "Hello. I'm Flurry. What's your name?"

The cats looked at each other and whispered amongst themselves. Then one of the cats took a few steps toward Flurry. This one had a red cape, a skull for his headpiece, and solid black fur which made his green eyes stand out more. "No! It is I who asks the questions! What are you doing here? This land is forbidden!" The cat crossed his arms and scowled.

"We're looking for the land of sour pies," Flurry replied.

"There's no such land!" the cat replied to him in a rude tone of voice.

"Uh huh! I have a map! See!" Flurry quickly brought forth the map. Two cats, that appeared to be the black cat's guards, crossed their spears in front of the bear cub. The black cat made a motion with his paw, which allowed Flurry to proceed. Without any hesitation, Flurry handed over the map.

"Flurry!" Fall called out. "You need to stop doing that! You're far too trusting of strangers!"

"Your map says land of the Sourpie."

"Yeah, that!"

"We are the Sourpie!"

"You may look sour, but you don't look like pies," Flurry answered.

The cat hissed at Flurry and his comrades and then went on. "Sourpie is the plural form of 'sourpuss'. We were given that name, along with the curse many ages ago."

"Curse? What curse?"

"You came all of the way here, from wherever you're from, and you don't know of the curse?"

"Uhm … No. I just came looking for pies. Do you have any? I'm starving!"

The cat which conversed with Flurry had the biggest headpiece on, which indicated that he was the leader. He stood there with a large ax in one paw. The black cat looked to the others, spoke something in an unknown language, and instantly a couple of the cats ran off. Only a short moment later, the cats returned with large plates containing various items of food.

"I hope these are satisfactory to you, for it's all that we have meow," the leader replied.

Flurry examined the edible offerings, but noticed they were not his first choice of food. One of the plates contained lemons, tamarinds, limes, and grapefruit. The other plate had an arrangement of bowls containing pickles and other fermented vegetables. To drink, the cats had sour milk.

"Yuck! Do you have anything else? I saw bananas in the trees earlier," Flurry inquired.

"Yes, we're aware of that, but we cannot

touch them. Any foods other than what you see here instantly become rotten when we touch them. We've been unable to eat anything else for many ages meow."

"Oh my! Don't touch me!" Fall's interruption was met with a disgusted look on the cat's face.

Not understanding, Flurry went on. "But! But! What about the pie? Where's the pie?"

Fall could not help but interrupt. "Flurry, there aren't any pies. Don't you see? You misunderstood. I tried to tell you! These cats ARE the Sourpie, and this is their land. There aren't any sweets."

"Oh! What about the cats in Tikalico? Do they have pie?" Flurry just could not let the matter rest.

Flurry's statement hit a nerve with the jungle's inhabitants. The cats hissed, and the fur on their backs stood up. "How do you know about them? It's against our laws to speak of them!" The king hastily turned and sent his order. "Quickly! Bind these intruders and bring them with us! They must be spies, sent by the others!"

The cats had them surrounded. They were too numerous for Flurry to count. They bound the arms and paws of the bear cubs with ropes made from vines, and led them through the jungle by the tip of their spears.

"Well, this is just great!" Fall shouted in Flurry's direction. "Thanks a lot, Flurry! You managed to get us in an even bigger mess now, didn't you?" Flurry grinned an uneasy, embarrassed grin. On the inside, he felt really ashamed, but his pride did not want him to look wrong, so he continued to pretend that he had everything under control.

Flurry and the others were marched into a courtyard and tied up to large stone pillars. All of the stone structures looked old, worn, and colorless. Some of it had been leveled to nothing but rubble. The king approached Flurry and his partners again. "Which of our siblings sent you?"

"I don't know what you're talking about. I don't even know your name," Flurry answered.

"My name is King Sourpuss, and I don't have time to play these games! I know you were sent from Tikalico to spy on us. Meow, tell me! What do they want? They've already taken everything from us. Are they here to make our lives even worse?" The king's voice was filled with rage.

Flurry kept silent. He did not know how

he should respond, and he did not want to make matters worse. However, things got worse without Flurry having needed to say or do anything.

"Not speaking, huh? Very well! If you won't tell me what I want to know, we shall hurt one of your friends. Which one shall it be? I think the female will go first." The king motioned with his paw, and some of the other cats cut Fall's ropes to free her from the pillar. They seized her and brought her to the king. Sourpuss leaned her over the flames.

Fall cried out, "Flurry! Help me!"

Flurry heart was pierced by his sister's grief. Despite his conflict with having a sister, even he could not allow something bad happen to her. Tears flowed down Flurry's face. "There has been a mistake.

We don't know those cats. We came here for pie. Please, let us go!"

Flurry's pleading fell on deaf ears. In fact, it only angered the king. Sourpuss pulled Fall back, clapped his paws, and two other cats came up and cut Flurry's ropes. Flurry thought that maybe they had decided to free him and his friends, but he was wrong. "You're to deliver a message to King Ja'gwar for me. Tell him that if he wants any of you to live, that he must lift the curse from my clowder."

Flurry was not sure what a clowder was, but Fall was well read. She knew that "clowder" was a term used to describe a group or a cluster of cats. However, considering that she was a captive, she would not be with Flurry when he had to deliver the message.

As he pointed to the east, King Sourpuss looked at Flurry and ordered him to go, saying, "He has until midnight tomorrow night to make his decision. Meow, go!"

Flurry quickly ran off in the direction the king pointed. Tears rolled down his cheeks. He felt horrible for what had transpired. The cub did not mean for any of it to happen. Flurry just wanted to go on an exciting adventure and to eat pie. Little did he know the kind of trouble he would get himself and his friends into.

Flurry ran through the brush, over the rocks, and under branches. The darkness made it hard for him to see where he was going, but thanks to the full moon, he had some light to help illuminate his path. However, his excessive crying made it even more difficult for him to see where he was running. Flurry's foot got snagged on a tree root, and he tripped. Before he knew it, he found himself tumbling down a hill. Head over heels he went. Dirt and rocks flew over his head as he slid to the bottom of the slope. This turn of events only upset Flurry further, and he bewailed even more.

"Why is this happening to me?" Flurry cried out loud. "Maybe I'm being punished for being so mean to my sister? I'm sorry!" Flurry shouted toward the sky. "I didn't mean to! I was sad, because I thought Mama and Papa didn't love me anymore." Flurry cried so loud that he could be heard for miles. He had never been so sad before. Flurry felt like a bad friend to Caboose and a terrible brother to Fall. On top of it all, his snowy fur was messed up, and he was covered in dirt. This had to be the worst day of Flurry's life. In fact, Flurry now agreed with Fall in that he, too, missed Mama and Papa and wanted to go home.

In the midst of his tears, Flurry looked up and saw an island in the distance. There was a long, stone bridge that led to the island, and which had a community that lived there. The city was lit up with the orange glow of open flames. Flurry wiped his tears away, straightened his scarf, brushed off the dirt, and said, "Pull yourself together, Flurry! You have to save your sister!" After a short pause, he added, "And find pie."

Flurry had mustered the courage he needed to press on and was now more determined than ever to right the wrongs of the previous few days. Flurry marched down through the jungle, out to the beach, and strode across the stone bridge to the island community of Tikalico.

Flurry approached the entrance to the city. There he was met by guards. These city guards greatly resembled the cats he had met in the land of the Sourpie. Even the architecture was essentially the same, only the buildings here well taken care of with vibrant hues of red, green, blue, yellow, and orange. Something very peculiar was taking place between the two feline communities, but Flurry could not quite figure out what the root of it was yet.

"Halt!" the guards exclaimed. "Who are you? State your business here!"

"It's just me, Flurry." His voice quivered as he spoke. He was still deeply saddened by the events that had transpired, and he worried for his sister. "I was sent here by King Grumpy Cat. He wants me to give a message to your king."

"Sorry! Nobody enters here! Return to where you came from!" the guards ordered.

Flurry would not take no for an answer. "You have to let me see the king! My sister's in danger. They're going to hurt her, if I don't talk to the king."

"That's not our problem! No means no! Meow leave!" the guards answered and then crossed their spears, which blocked the way to the entrance. "This is your final warning. Leave meow, or we'll consider your presence an act of hostility toward our clowder, and we'll have you arrested."

Flurry was unwilling to budge. He crossed his arms and sat down on the stone floor outside the entrance to Tikalico. He was determined to save his sister and Caboose.

"Fine! Have it your way!" The guards approached Flurry with their spears pointed right at him. They seized him and dragged him along as they entered the city.

While Flurry was escorted into the city, he had plenty of chances to look at everything they passed by. The city was magnificent and beautiful. The stone structures were built with such mastery and precision. In addition to this, Flurry could smell food. The warm, delicious aromas saturated the air. Flurry's tummy grumbled which reminded him that he had not eaten since he left the company of the wolves. He was certain that this group of cats definitely had tasty treats such as pies – after all, that is why he came all that way.

Flurry found himself being led into a courtyard, much like the one he had just been in, back in the land of the Sourpie. The difference being that this courtyard had such majestic beauty to behold while the Sourpie's courtyard looked to be neglected and in ruins.

Before long, an important-looking cat with a large headdress came to meet him. His fur was yellow with black spots all over, and he had a big belly covered in white fur. "Who's this?" the cat asked the guards.

"Sire! We don't know. He says his name is Flurry. He insisted on speaking to you, and when we refused, he just sat at the entrance to our city and wouldn't leave," the guards answered.

The leader then turned to Flurry to address him. "Is this true?"

"Yes," Flurry replied.

"Then why are you here?"

Tears filled Flurry's eyes. "It's all my fault! I found this map to the land of the Sourpie. I thought it was a place to get pie and other tasty treats. But then they got my sister and my friend. They told me that if I don't give a message to you, they'll hurt them. I can't let that happen."

"What are their demands?" asked the black-spotted, yellow cat with the red and green headdress.

"They told me that they want King Ja'gwar to lift some kind of a curse."

The cat's eyes widened, and Flurry now had his full attention. "Really? That's what they said?"

"Uh huh," Flurry nodded his head and attempted to wipe away some of his tears.

"Well, I'm King Ja'gwar, and this is a very clever ploy they've crafted. This only goes to show that they haven't changed. After all of these years, they're the same savages they used to be!" The king turned his back and walked away.

Flurry was still uncertain what was going on. "Excuse me! Excuse me!" Flurry addressed the guards that stood next to him.

"Keep silent! The king has yet to decide what to do with you," the guards snapped back at Flurry.

"But I have a question."

"So what? Keep silent! We don't care what you have to say!"

"But …" Flurry's sentence stopped short when one of the guards pointed a spear at his face.

"Wait a minute! We could at least hear his question. It doesn't mean we have to answer it," the second guard told the first one, who still stood there with his spear tip nearly touching Flurry's nose.

"Fine! What do you want?" the spear-wielder asked as he pulled his weapon away from the bear cub.

"Why don't you and the Sourpie get along?"

"How could you not know this story? It's ages old," the guard replied.

"I'm not from around here. I'm from Ursus."

"Really? You're from the north? So you must know of Christopher Kringle!" the guards answered in unison.

The demeanor of the guards quickly changed. The two relaxed their posture, and they now seemed more friendly and cooperative toward Flurry. "Why didn't you tell us this before?" the spear-holder asked.

He turned to the other guard and said, "Quickly, run and tell the king that this bear comes from Christopher Kringle's land."

The other cat ran off on all fours, instead of only his hind legs. The cat guard was very quick. He was out of sight before the remaining guard was able to turn back to face Flurry.

"Since you aren't from around here, I'll tell you the story. Once, both of our clowders were one. In fact, we all lived here in Tikalico together. It was a prosperous time, and we had the protection of the twin necklaces."

"Necklaces?" Flurry asked.

"Yes, but one of them is now lost to us. The king and his brother once ruled together. Things were good, but the king's brother was secretly jealous of him. His jealousy grew to the point of hatred. One day, the traitorous brother led a rebellion against our king and tried to overthrow him so he could have this kingdom for himself. King Ja'gwar was victorious in the battle, but his brother wouldn't hand over the necklace after his defeat. Instead, he made a pact with a pack of wolves to help him defeat us in a second battle.

"The wolves agreed to help him, but for a price. The wolves demanded his necklace in exchange for their help. When Sourpuss agreed to this, the wolves betrayed him and took the necklace for themselves without keeping their end of the bargain. I guess it's only fitting since Sourpuss betrayed us. I suppose he got a taste of his own medicine."

"What's so great about these necklaces, anyway?"

"The two necklaces have special powers. We don't fully understand how they work. Our king's necklace protects our community, and the second necklace provides long life and strength to its wearer. However, when both necklaces are brought together, they spread long life and protection to everyone in the city. If someone had both necklaces and kept them for themselves, they could essentially be immortal."

Curious to know more, Flurry inquired further. "So why do the Sourpie not live here anymore? Oh! And why are they called Sourpie? They don't look like pies, though they do have the 'sour' part down pretty well."

"Because of their bad attitudes and their poisonous nature, our leader gave his brother the name 'Sourpuss' and crowned him as King of the Sourpie. They eventually embraced that name and meow act proud of it. Sourpie is simply the plural form of sourpuss."

"Ohhh … I see."

"They were banished to the ruined city of Agrio in the wildest part of the jungle with a curse placed upon them. The curse won't allow them to taste anything sweet ever again. They may only eat or drink that which is sour or rotten, as a punishment for their evil."

"Is there any way to break the curse?" Flurry sounded deeply concerned.

"Only our king has the power to do that, and he won't do so. He cannot allow their crimes to go unpunished."

"But you said this happened a long time ago. Shouldn't they forgive each other and forget?"

"They are of the same litter. Sometimes, it can be very hard for siblings to get along. It is said that the more you love someone, the deeper the pain can be when you feel betrayed by them. I don't foresee our two clowders becoming one ever again. At least not in my lifetime."

Flurry looked down at the ground. He now felt even guiltier for how he had treated his sister. He saw how his own jealousy had made him a sourpuss, too. Flurry felt it should be him being held captive by the Sourpie, not his sister. Flurry wept as remorse consumed his thoughts.

"What's wrong?" asked the guard.

"Everything's my fault!" Flurry replied. "If I hadn't been jealous of my sister, none of this would've happened."

"Don't fret, poor Flurry, for I'll help you," came a voice in the distance. Flurry looked up and saw the guard return with the king. Flurry had not noticed before, but around the king's neck was the other necklace. It appeared much like that which Isangrim wore, but it had a purple gemstone instead of red. The king continued. "I don't believe the Sourpie are worthy to have the curse lifted, as demonstrated by their actions. However, I won't allow our rivalry with the Sourpie to doom innocent lives. First thing tomorrow morning, we shall travel to the camp of the Sourpie and rescue your friend and your sister from their clutches."

CHAPTER 6
BETRAYED

Throughout the night, Flurry was treated like a prince. The king pulled out all of the stops to attend to Flurry's needs and make sure he was comfortable. Delicious foods of many types were prepared, but Flurry had lost his appetite. All Flurry could think of was his sister and Caboose. His mind was focused on their rescue. Flurry could not sleep. He tossed and turned the night away until morning finally arrived.

There was a knock at his door, and the

king entered, along with his royal guards that protected him from all forms of danger. "Flurry, my guest, did you sleep well?"

"Not really," Flurry answered with a frown on his face.

"Well, cheer up, the time is at hand. Bring whatever you need and meet us in the courtyard. Our journey begins meow. Let's go save your friend and your sister from the evil Sourpie." The king clapped his paws, and his guards followed him out the door.

Flurry hopped down from the bed and quickly trailed close behind. In the courtyard, dozens of warriors were armed and ready to go. Their caravan set out across the bridge in the direction of Agrio. Little did any of them realize that they were being spied upon by the wolves that Isangrim had sent out ahead. "It looks like our plan is proceeding just as Isangrim expected." The wolves looked at each other and chuckled before running on ahead of the feline travelers.

The wolves made hast to meet up with two other wolf scouts. "Tell Isangrim that King Ja'gwar is on the move," said the leader of the three that arrived from Tikalico. "It looks like he's heading to Agrio. If Isangrim moves quickly enough, he can cut them off at the mountain pass." The wolf scouts nodded and ran off, while the original three turned back toward Tikalico.

The king, his troops, and Flurry were now deep in the jungle and were closing in on the Sourpie camp. Flurry felt good about himself. He was about to see his friend and sister rescued, and they could return home and pretend the past few days had never happened. Flurry was ready for it to be over. He had learned his lesson about jealousy and how it could cause him to make foolish decisions.

As the company pushed forward up the mountain, they came upon a pass. The guards then warned the king, "Sire! It's unwise to pass this way. It's a strategically inferior position, if the Sourpie decide to ambush us."

The king took note, but ordered them forward anyway. As they moved through the pass, the king answered the guard privately, "You're correct, but with my necklace, it would be a fool's errand for the Sourpie to attempt to attack us."

Suddenly, a loud booming voice spoke from above. "Maybe it would be for them, but not for me." Flurry looked around, but could not see where the voice came from, though he did find it to be very familiar.

The king's guards formed a perimeter around their ruler and Flurry as they stood ready for battle. They all looked to and fro in search of the origin of the voice. Then they saw the large, menacing form of Jarl Isangrim the Great as he stood high above them.

"It's an ambush!" yelled the guards.

"Indeed, it is!" Isangrim answered. "But it doesn't have to end badly. I'm a reasonable wolf after all."

The other wolves, in hiding, chuckled as they revealed themselves one-by-one. The king, his warriors, and Flurry were surrounded by Pack Isangrim. All of the wolves had the high ground, which gave them the advantage. Despite this fact, the king did not seem concerned. He knew that his necklace would protect them. He turned toward his companions and said, "Gather close to me. They cannot harm us while I have my necklace."

"On the contrary!" Isangrim began, as he leapt down from the rock and strolled toward the brave company of warrior cats. "You're going to hand the necklace over to me, or else you'll be the cause of the downfall of Tikalico. I have sent members of my pack out ahead. They await my signal. Be careful what you do; it could cost you the lives of your clowder."

The king was speechless. He could not believe what was happening. His mind raced for answers, and the only conclusion he could come up with was that his brother somehow had made another pact with the wolves and had planned this all along.

"Don't do it!" Flurry shouted.

The king, knowing that he had been outwitted, stepped forward, removed his necklace, and began to hand it to Isangrim. "It's yours, if you give me your word that you'll not harm my clowder."

"Oh, I give you no word. The way I look at it, you don't have a choice. Hand it over, and I give you my word that you'll have less of a casualty list than if you don't. That's the only word I offer," Isangrim replied.

Isangrim paused for a moment, but when he noticed Ja'gwar's continued reluctance he added, "However, if hearing the words will help make the decision easier for you, then I promise that none of your clowder will be harmed this day."

"The word of a wolf? I never thought it would come to this." The king closed his eyes, turned his head away, and handed the necklace to Isangrim.

Isangrim laughed. "Now was that so hard?"

Flurry could not believe what was happening. Fall was right. Isangrim was bad! Flurry felt foolish and upset that he had been tricked. In an attempt to help, Flurry spoke up in protest. "Hey! I thought you were a friend! How could you do this? How could you? How could you?"

"Ha, ha, ha, ha, ha!" laughed Isangrim. "Foolish bear, you're the one to blame for being so naïve. I told you what you wanted to hear. But look on the bright side; you spared this cat countless losses today. You should be proud."

All of the wolves laughed and pointed at Flurry and the others. "Now, if you'll excuse me, I have to plan our raid. We've got to eat, you know," Isangrim taunted.

"Wait a minute! You said you wouldn't harm my clowder!" King Ja'gwar shouted. "I knew I shouldn't have trusted your word!"

"Correction, fur ball! I said I would spare them today. I made no promises about tomorrow. Besides, the meal I'm referring to is that of the Sourpie. Now that I have the necklace, I can lift the curse and make a meal out of them. You should be thanking me. I'm finally ridding you of your treacherous brother," Isangrim taunted just before he ran off into the jungle with the rest of his wolves that followed after him. The wolves howled and laughed as they departed.

Wolfhroc paused for a moment and looked down at them. Flurry sensed a tinge of remorse upon her face. Flurry thought he would try to get through to her. "I thought we were friends. Please, help us!"

"You're wasting your breath. Isangrim is my jarl and my husband. I cannot go against his wishes," Wolfhroc answered him and then ran off with the others.

"What have I done?" cried the king, as he fell to all fours in tears. He turned to Flurry and said, "I only meant to help you, but meow my entire clowder is doomed. We have no protection against the wolves. Even with our numbers being greater, we can't match the size, strength, and speed of the wolves. What ever shall we do?" The king buried his face in his paws and sobbed uncontrollably.

Flurry came up to the king's side and whispered in his ear, "Mister Cat, I don't mean to be rude, but shouldn't we stop them? We should make a plan to save everyone. Also, you're the king. Maybe you shouldn't cry in front of everyone."

The king looked up, wiped the tears from his eyes, and stood back up. With a more dignified posture, he turned to address Flurry. "You're very brave for such a little bear. I admire this, but you don't know what you suggest. The odds are greatly stacked against us. I'm not sure where to even begin."

"Well, first, you should make up with your brother," Flurry answered.

"Not a chance! Do you know what he did to me and my clowder?"

"Yes, but he's your brother! Can't you forget about your pride and forgive each other?" *Now I see why Santa was concerned about my pride*, Flurry thought to himself.

"I like your attitude. You have hope and bravery, and those are good things to have. However, you're too idealistic. Not everyone is willing to throw away their hard feelings and move on. Some cats just can't let go."

"Well, you should be the better cat and do it first. Maybe it'll catch on."

The king was impressed. A hint of a smile appeared on his face. "Perhaps you're right. I'll give it a try."

"If you and your brother become friends again, he could join us against the big, bad wolves. They won't see it coming."

The king smiled at Flurry and turned to

his warriors to give them their commands. "The six of you will go out ahead of us to Tikalico. Warn everyone to seek shelter, take up arms, and prepare for an attack. Make sure to fortify the city the best you can." Then he turned to some of his other warriors. "You three, track the wolves. Find out where their camp is and find out anything you can about their plans, strengths, and weaknesses. The rest of you shall accompany Flurry and me to meet with my brother." Without a moment's hesitation, each group took off to carry out the king's orders.

It was not long before Flurry and King Ja'gwar arrived at the camp of the Sourpie. By this point rays from the sun shone directly down from above. The leader of the Sourpie came out to see his brother. "So you've come. I didn't think you could let an innocent soul perish. You're so predictable, even after all of these years."

"Well, I hate to be the bearer of bad news, but I cannot lift the curse. My necklace has been stolen by Isangrim, the wolf," King Ja'gwar replied.

"What? Unacceptable! All you've done is doom yourself along with our other prisoners! Guards! Arrest them!"

"Wait, brother! You're making a grave mistake!"

"Oh, am I? For all I know, it was you who told the wolves to betray us the first time and take our necklace. You probably have both of them, and you're just lying to me about it meow."

"That's not true! We came here to save you. We're here to warn you that the wolves are planning to attack your clowder."

"They cannot, or the curse will be upon them, too. If you're going to lie, you need to do better than that."

"No, that's just it! Don't you see? With my necklace, they can lift the curse and then devour all of you. But if our clowders combine, we might be strong enough to repel an attack."

King Sourpuss paused for a moment and then replied, "We're not strong enough to hold off such an attack, not without the combined strength of the necklaces. It would be foolish to take on Isangrim without them."

"United we stand, but divided we'll fall. Please set aside the past. Don't you see that being brothers is more important than any wrongs we might have caused each other?"

King Ja'gwar tried to plead and reason with Sourpuss, but to no end. His brother would not listen and had them tied up to the stone columns, right next to Caboose and Fall. As King Sourpuss walked away, his brother shouted, "I forgive you!" The statement angered Sourpuss as he stormed off in haste.

Flurry was a clever little fellow. He had snuck off into the jungle while the brothers argued. Nobody had even noticed his absence. Flurry ran as fast as his little feet would carry him. He ran until he came across one of King Ja'gwar's warriors that had been tracking the wolves. "I'm so glad to see you!" Flurry panted, while he tried to catch his breath to continue his message. "King Ja'gwar and the others have been captured by Sourpatch."

"I must get my companions and go save

him right away!" answered the warrior.

"No, wait!" Flurry called out as he grabbed the cat's paw. "We need a plan, and I think I have just the one!"

Flurry whispered in the cat's ear for a good while. After he finished, the cat nodded and replied, "I think your plan will work. Hurry! We must move quickly!" They both ran off into the jungle toward the camp of the Sourpie. Flurry's plan was time sensitive, so they did not bother to recruit the other warriors to come with them.

The arrived just outside the ruins. Flurry could see the captives. He and the warrior cat snuck in without being detected. It was not difficult. King Sourpuss believed he had all of them tied up. There was no reason to keep a close eye on them. Flurry cut Fall and Caboose's ropes and gave each of them a hug. Caboose was overjoyed and hung on to Flurry for a prolonged length of time.

"You're clear! Go meow!" said the cat warrior. "I'll rescue the king and the other cats. You need to stop Isangrim!"

"Roger!" Flurry replied and ran off into the jungle, closely followed by Fall and Caboose.

"Do you think he'll be okay?" asked Fall.

"I'm sure he'll be fine," Flurry answered.

"Where did you learn how to use procedure words, like 'roger'?" Fall asked.

Confused, Flurry answered, "Huh? His name is Roger."

"Oh …" came Fall's surprised response.

"Get down! We're close to Isangrim's camp." Flurry spoke in a whisper. He crawled up to a grassy mound that concealed them from sight as they overlooked the camp. Not being a real bear, Flurry did not have a scent that was strong enough for the wolves to pick up on and be alerted to his presence.

Flurry watched the wolves as they prepared for battle. In the distance, Flurry could see that Isangrim still wore his necklace with the red gemstone. The other necklace, with the purple gemstone, hung from Wolfhroc's neck.

While the bear cubs were crouched close to the ground, one of the warrior cats stealthily approached them. Flurry quickly filled him in on their plan and informed the little warrior how he intended to get the necklaces back. The warrior then ran off to tell the other cat of their plan before going into hiding to wait for their moment to come.

"Flurry, that takes care of everything except for the necklace that Isangrim is wearing. What will we do about that one?" Fall asked.

Flurry patted her on the shoulder and said, "No need to worry, I think I have just the thing!"

CHAPTER 7
FLURRY'S PLAN

Isangrim stood proud as he watched the other wolves prepare for battle. Though he had the necklaces to protect the pack, he did not want to take any chances. As the wolves put their armor on, Isangrim heard a voice in the distance. The voice grew louder as it drew nearer.

Isangrim turned and saw Fall run into the camp. "Oh, my! Oh, my! Flurry has been captured by the Sourpie!" Fall continued to repeat as she ran up to Isangrim.

Isangrim looked her over and asked, "What difference is that to me?"

"What do you mean? I thought we were your friends."

"Dear, you're late to the party. I already got what I needed, without Flurry's help. Now go! Get lost!"

"Please! Can't you help him? If you do this, I'll be eternally grateful to you. Then we'll be out of your way for good."

"No! When I rip you to shreds, then you'll be out of my way for good!" Isangrim growled.

"Now, husband, please be kind to her. She meant no disrespect," Wolfhroc intervened.

Isangrim quickly shot an angry glare in his wife's direction. "You! Stay out of this!"

Just then, Isangrim's lookout howled.

Clearly irritated, Isangrim growled, "What is it now?"

"Another wolf approaches!" the lookout called down.

"Everyone's here! What other wolf could it be? Who is it?"

"I don't know. I don't recognize him. He looks rather elderly, if I do say so myself."

Sure enough, an extremely old wolf meandered into Isangrim's camp. This particular wolf was so thin that it appeared to be nothing but fur and bones. He did not walk well either. However, little did they know that this wolf was part of Flurry's ploy. Inside the costume was Caboose, on stilts. It was Caboose's job to distract Isangrim while Fall tried to get his necklace.

As Caboose approached in his poorly-made costume, Isangrim circled him with caution. The jarl of Pack Isangrim was suspicious. He sniffed and examined the frail visitor.

"Who, may I ask, are you?" Isangrim inquired.

"I'm a wolf," Caboose answered.

"I can see that. Though you've got to be the ugliest wolf I've ever seen."

"Oh, sank you!" lisped Caboose.

Isangrim shook his head. "That wasn't a compliment." The pack's leader raised his voice. "Your name! What's your name?" Isangrim's frustration and lack of patience was abundantly evident.

Caboose could not think of one. Flurry had not planned that part out. From a distance, Flurry watched to make sure their plans did not go awry. When Isangrim became distracted by Caboose, Flurry was going to make a run for the necklace Wolfhroc wore.

As Flurry watched, worrisome thoughts set in. He became increasingly concerned by the answers Caboose kept giving to Isangrim. Flurry was certain that they were going to be found out.

Caboose attempted to think of a name in vain, and he blurted out, "My name is Wolfy McWolfington from suh Turnip pack."

Isangrim's mouth dropped open as he stared at Caboose with disbelief. "I've never heard of such a pack. If it exists, that has to be the worst name I've ever heard! You look like you could fall over dead at any moment. You don't look healthy at all."

"Well, you know, unhealssy is suh new healssy."

Isangrim stood up straight and shook his

head in disbelief. Flurry did likewise and buried his face in his paws. "Oh, Caboose!" Flurry muttered, followed by a sigh.

It was this moment Isangrim was convinced that something was definitely wrong. He sniffed around Caboose again. "Oh no! He knows!" Flurry whispered to himself, as he watched in fear. Flurry knew this was the "now or never" moment, so he signaled the other two cats that hid among the trees.

Isangrim grabbed ahold of the elderly wolf's fur and gave it a tug. The fur fell to the ground and revealed Caboose as he stood there on stilts.

"Hello!" Caboose cheerfully greeted the jarl.

An arrow flew at Isangrim's head and grazed the back of his neck. It appeared to be a near miss, but the purpose of the arrow was a success. The shot caused Isangrim's necklace to fall to the ground.

Fall used her foot to quickly cover the necklace with the fur from Caboose's costume, so Isangrim would not see it lying there.

Another arrow did likewise as it grazed the back of Wolfhroc's neck. "We're under attack!" shouted Isangrim. "You two! You're a part of this somehow, I just know it! You're coming with me!"

"Not if you want this!" Flurry called out from the ridgeline. The cub held up one of the necklaces.

"You! How did you get that?" Isangrim then reached for his own to find it missing as well. He quickly spun around and glared at Fall and Caboose. He was certain they were the culprits. Isangrim postured himself to pounce the cubs. He bared his teeth and growled at the two cubs.

They probably would have been ripped to shreds if the second part of Flurry's plan had not worked. As Isangrim was about to attack Fall and Caboose, a horn sounded, and an army of cats appeared from all sides of the camp. Spears and arrows littered the sky as the attack commenced.

Normally, such an attack would not have worried Isangrim, but he was without both of the necklaces, and the cats from Tikalico were accompanied by the Sourpie as well. It stood to reason that King Sourpuss and King Ja'gwar had resolved their differences. The brothers stood side-by-side as they watched the battle commence.

"How could this have happened?"

Isangrim asked himself as he ran for cover from the arrows. He looked up and saw Flurry run toward the kings with one of the necklaces. Isangrim broke from cover, ran toward Flurry, and shouted, "You! You did this! If I can't win this battle, I can at least have the satisfaction of ripping you apart!" Isangrim leapt at Flurry with his maw wide open, teeth bared, and claws extended. It appeared to be the end of Flurry.

Flurry screamed and fell to the ground with his eyes covered. The cub did not want to see the fate that was about to befall him. A moment or two passed, but Flurry did not feel like he was being ripped apart. The bear cub decided to peek out and see what had happened. There he beheld Isangrim frozen in midair by the power of the necklace. Flurry had held the necklace up over his head to shield himself from the wolf's attack.

"Put me down!" Isangrim demanded. "Face me like a true warrior! I challenge you! Only a coward would hide behind that necklace."

Flurry stood up and bravely replied, "Oh, so that's why you wore one?"

Isangrim growled and looked upon Flurry with eyes full of rage.

While Flurry and Isangrim struggled, Fall grabbed the other necklace from the ground and ran toward the cat kings in the hope of getting it to them, but her path was blocked by Wolfhroc. "Where do you think you're going with that?" asked the she wolf.

"Please! How can you be like this? I thought you were our friend," Fall replied.

"You and your brother need to do a better

job at picking your friends." Suddenly Wolfhroc's mouth opened wide. She revealed her razor-like teeth and bit down on the bear cub. Fall screamed as Wolfhroc lifted her up by the back of her neck.

The next moments did not play out as Fall thought they would. She opened her eyes and saw herself being carried by Wolfhroc up to King Sourpuss. The wolf dropped Fall at his feet. "Don't tell Isangrim that I helped you, and don't expect any favors from me in the future. This was a one-time deal." Wolfhroc then turned and ran off with the other wolves. They had retreated due to the overwhelming number of cats and the fact that the feline warriors now had both of the necklaces for protection.

The kings and the most elite guards closed in on Flurry and Isangrim. They both had been frozen in place, but for Flurry it was out of sheer fright.

"I give you the opportunity to surrender or to perish right here." The king of Tikalico addressed Isangrim, while he removed the necklace from Flurry's paw and put it back around his own neck where it belonged. He then released Isangrim from the necklace's hold.

"Never! I'll never surrender!" Isangrim snarled.

"Very well. Have it your way," The king replied. "Archers! Take aim!"

Isangrim, though defeated, was still very strong and extremely fast. He leapt at the cats, knocking many of them down, and ran into the jungle. The wolf disappeared behind a wall of vines and other vegetation.

"Pursue him!" the king ordered, and a

legion of cats ran into the jungle in hot pursuit.

Flurry approached the kings. "I'm glad you can both be friends again."

"It's all thanks to you, young one," said King Ja'gwar. "You have a lot of wisdom for such a young age. We did as you suggested, and I appealed to my brother again. So, as of this very moment the curse has been lifted, and the Sourpie are no more." Ja'gwar then turned to his brother. "You shall no longer be named Sourpuss, and your clowder are meow citizens of Tikalico." Everyone cheered. The cats lifted Flurry, Fall, and Caboose into the air, and carried them around as heroes of the battle.

That night, festivities reigned, and Flurry was finally getting all of the tasty treats he had come all that way for. On Flurry's table he had every kind of pie imaginable, not to mention his plates of cookies and cakes. Flurry scarfed down his food so fast that it appeared to vanish into thin air. With crumbs all over his fur he shouted, "Yum! Yum!"

Every story has an end, so that a new adventure can begin. And with all stories, this one had now come to an end, too. In the morning, Flurry, Fall, and Caboose were given miniature ponies to ride upon, and an armed division of Tikalico warriors were sent with them to protect and accompany the cubs back to Ursus.

"Thank you for all of the tasty food!" Flurry exclaimed to the two kings.

"No, it is we who should thank you. If not for you, our two clowders may never have been reunited. You, your family, and your friends will always be welcome here. Have a safe journey back," King Ja'gwar replied.

Everyone cheered, and confetti rained down from above while Flurry, Fall, and Caboose were led out of the city, across the bridge, and on their way back home.

After they rode for a little while, Fall turned to Flurry and said, "You know what? You're not such a bad brother after all."

Flurry blushed. "Thanks, but I was a bad brother. I'm sorry that I was so mean to you. I'm also sorry for being jealous. You're not such a bad sister either." Then he turned to look at Caboose and said, "And you do a great wolf act!" Flurry giggled.

"Sank you!" Caboose replied. "What's a wolf?"

Fall laughed. Flurry buried his face in his paws. The siblings learned that family and love are what truly matter, and they felt happy to have each other. Along with Caboose, the three of them giggled and laughed all the way home.

EPILOGUE
ISANGRIM'S PLEDGE

Nightfall had come, and Pack Isangrim were huddled up in their cave near the southeastern shore, beyond the mountain range the enclosed the feline territory. It was quite a distance from the jungle out of which they had been chased.

In the infamous cavern known as Isangrand, Jarl Isangrim the Great sat on his throne which had been chiseled from solid stone. Bones were scattered all over the floor of the cave. Wolfhroc lay at the foot of the throne, below Isangrim's feet.

As they exchanged glances, Isangrim's face twitched with rage. His eyes were wide, and his teeth showed as he growled.

He suddenly stood up, shoved one of the wolves from his path, strolled to the mouth of the cave, and looked out over the enormous lake. Thunder shook the walls of the cave as dark and ominous storm clouds were seen above the water along the distant horizon. Wolfhroc came to her spouse's side in an attempt to comfort him. "What is it that troubles you, husband?"

Without a reaction to her presence or breaking his glare from the violent waves, he replied, "This isn't over! Mark my words! I'll have my revenge, if it's the last thing I do. I shall find Flurry and make him suffer for what he has done to me!"

Lightning bolted down from the clouds, and a loud crack of thunder shook the cave just as a female voice spoke from the shadows behind him. "Perhaps I may be of assistance."

Isangrim turned and looked in the direction of the voice. He recognized the silhouette of the feline figure coming out from the shadows. With a hint of disdain in Isangrim's expression, he asked, "For what purpose does an assassin stand in my presence?"

The female cat stepped into the torch-lit opening. She had golden fur and sparkling green eyes. "You know who I am!" she remarked. "Necatual, or Necat, will suffice, thank you." An evil smirk appeared upon her furry face. She felt proud of her wit before such a ferocious beast.

"As you already know, King Ja'gwar wiped out my great city many years ago, killing my family and all that I loved. I intended to use the Sourpie in my scheme to overthrow him. That bear cub thwarted my plans, too. If we join forces, we can both have what we want."

Isangrim looked away from Necatual and turned his gaze out toward the storm. The wolf's posture straightened, his eyes narrowed, and a grin came to his mouth. Without breaking his gaze upon the waves, he replied, "The enemy of my enemy is my friend indeed!"

ABOUT J.S. SKYE

J.S. Skye grew up in the Midwestern region of the United States. At a very young age, it was apparent that he was very talented. Finding that he was gifted in music and art, he plunged himself into both. As time passed, he set aside music to focus even more of his attention on developing his skills as an illustrator.

All throughout his years in school, J.S. Skye spent every available moment creating and developing fictional worlds. Caring about realism, he developed multiple people groups, countries, worlds, and even languages. His fictional realms were created through both written and visual mediums.

After traveling to almost a dozen different countries and studying different cultures, J.S. Skye decided to implement his interests in ancient cultures, history, languages, mythology, and more into his writings. He decided it was best to pour his heart and passion into writing instead of having divided interests between both art and literature.

J.S. Skye has accumulated a fairly large collection of his various writings. These stories range from all types of different genres such as mystery, science fiction, fantasy, and even horror. Friends encouraged the aspiring writer to produce a novel and see how things progressed from there.

J.S. Skye's first novel, *The Granted Wish*, was met with cheerful affirmation. The positive feedback was overwhelming and unexpected. Fans of his *Flurry the Bear* novels grew and began to clamor for more. From this point forward, his first novel series came to be.

For more information or to get in touch with J.S. Skye personally, he may be contacted by e-mail at:

JS-Skye@FlurryTheBear.com

ALSO BY J.S. SKYE

Flurry the Bear – The Granted Wish

Flurry the Bear – The Throne of Frost

Flurry the Bear – The Book of Snow

Flurry the Bear – The Rising Tide